UNWIN HYMA ___ S

STE___C

OUT

INCLUDING
FOLLOW ON
ACTIVITIES

EDITED BY JANE LEGGETT

Unwin Hyman Short Stories
Openings   edited by Roy Blatchford
Round Two   edited by Roy Blatchford
School's OK   edited by Josie Karavasil and Roy Blatchford
Stepping Out   edited by Jane Leggett
That'll Be The Day   edited by Roy Blatchford
Sweet and Sour   edited by Gervase Phinn
It's Now or Never   edited by Jane Leggett and Roy Blatchford
Pigs is Pigs   edited by Trevor Millum
Dreams and Resolutions   edited by Roy Blatchford

Unwin Hyman Collections
Free As I Know   edited by Beverley Naidoo
Solid Ground   edited by Jane Leggett and Sue Libovitch
In Our Image   edited by Andrew Goodwyn

Unwin Hyman Plays
Stage Write   edited by Gervase Phinn

Published by
UNWIN HYMAN LIMITED
15/17 Broadwick Street
London W1V 1FP

Selection and notes © Roy Blatchford and Jane Leggett 1987
The copyright of each story remains the property of the author

Reprinted 1988

British Library Cataloguing in Publication Data

Unwin Hyman short stories for GCSE Vol.B
   1. Short stories, English   2. English fiction –
   20th century
   I. Leggett, Jane
   823'01'08 [FS]   PR1309.S5

   ISBN 0–7135–2712–9

Typeset by Typecast Limited, Tonbridge
Printed and bound in Great Britain by Billing & Sons Ltd. Worcester

Series cover design by Iain Lanyon
Cover illustration by Chris Najman © 1987

Contents

Acknowledgements

The editor and publishers wish to thank the following for permission to reprint the short stories:

The Women's Press Ltd for 'Raymond's Run' by Toni Cade Bambara from *Gorilla My Love and other stories*, published by The Women's Press Ltd, 1984, and Random House, New York.

McIntosh and Otis, Inc., New York for 'Flame on the Frontier' by Dorothy M. Johnson, from the collection *Indian Country*, Ballantine Books. © Dorothy M. Johnson 1978.

Centerprise Trust Ltd for 'The Ugliest of Them All' by Stella Ibekwe from the collection *Teenage Encounters*, Centerprise Trust, 1978.

Laura Cecil (Literary Agent) for 'Snapshots of Paradise' by Adèle Geras from the collection *Snapshots of Paradise*, Athenuem, New York. Personal essay © Adèle Geras, 1986.

Don Congdon Associates Inc., New York for 'Debut' by Kristin Hunter published in *Negro Digest*, June 1968. © Kristin Hunter, 1968.

Olywomen Press Ltd for 'The Kestrels' by Kym Martindale, originally published in *The Reach: Lesbian feminist fiction*, edited by Lilian Mohin and Sheila Shulman, Onlywomen Press, 1984.

Sheba Feminist Publishers for 'The Application Form' by Moy McCrory from *The Water's Edge*, Sheba Feminist Publishers, 1985. Personal essay © Moy McCrory, 1986.

Jonathan Cape Ltd for 'A Chip of Glass Ruby' by Nadine Gordimer from *Selected Stories*, Jonathan Cape, 1976.

Henry Holt and Company, Inc., New York for 'Gawain and the Lady Ragnell' by Ethel Johnston Phelps from *The Maid of the North*, retold by Ethel Johnston Phelps. © 1981 by Ethel Johnston Phelps. Reprinted by permission of Henry Holt and Company.

Introduction

Fiction has always been a major resource for teachers and students involved in the study of language and literature. Perhaps its most important contribution has been the enjoyment and pleasure that readers gain. Equally, fiction has been used because of its power to engage attention and the imagination, and give shape to personal experiences and expectations.

Many of the issues we wish to discuss with students are complex, challenging and probing. Reading fiction provides a chance to consider and reflect on them from a distance, before moving into the realm of personal experience and opinion. Fiction also offers a wealth of models of writing and expression which can be used to assist students in their own writing.

The aim of this collection is to provide a resource for students studying English and English Literature for the General Certificate of Secondary Education.

The stories have been selected first and foremost because they are fine examples of the short story genre, and are perhaps best enjoyed when read aloud and shared with a group of students. But they also offer opportunities to talk and write about issues that are of concern and relevance to young people.

All the stories in *Stepping Out* are written by women and most have strong and independent central female characters. A particular feature of the collection is that most of the stories end on a positive note: not necessarily the traditional 'happy ending', but an ending in which expectations and perceptions – of both the reader *and* the characters in the story – have changed.

Opening the volume is 'Raymond's Run', an engaging, witty story of rivalry and friendship. In other stories such as 'The Kestrels', 'Turned' and 'Gawain and the Lady Ragnell' themes of friendship and independence are further explored.

'Snapshots of Paradise', previously unpublished in this country, is a lighthearted story which examines with humour and sensitivity the beginnings of boy-girl friendship and romance. The images that girls have of themselves during adolescence are examined in different ways in 'The Ugliest of Them All' and 'Debut'. The theme of parent/child conflict introduced in 'Debut' is pursued in 'The Application Form'. Women as individuals and as mothers are powerfully portrayed in these two stories and in 'A Chip of Glass Ruby'.

'Flame on the Frontier' concerns the different social and cultural expectations of early white American settlers and the Sioux Indians.

The collection concludes with perhaps the most challenging story, a compelling and disturbing narrative about incipient insanity. This may seem a melancholy note on which to end, but it is not: its author wrote of the story: 'It was not intended to drive people crazy, but to save people from being driven crazy and it worked'.

The volume also includes personal essays by Adèle Geras and Moy McCrory which serve to illuminate their own stories and the short story genre. Students will find these valuable both in their personal writing and in studying the genre.

The range of 'Follow On' activities is designed to present a variety of talking and writing assignments that will help students to gain in confidence and competence at using language effectively in any context. They also offer a range of approaches which will help students of all abilities, whether in building up a coursework folder or in preparing for essays written under examination conditions. More specifically, the activities aim to encourage students to:

▶ work independently and collaboratively
▶ consider:
  – the short story as genre
  – language and style of a writer
  – structure and development of plot
  – development of character
  – setting
▶ examine the writer's viewpoint and intentions
▶ respond critically and imaginatively to the stories, orally and in writing
▶ read a variety of texts, including quite difficult ones
▶ read more widely.

One important footnote: the activities are divided under three broad headings – *Before*; *During*; *After Reading*. The intention is that students should engage with the text as closely as possible, from predicting storylines to analysing characters' motivations. Teachers using this collection are therefore recommended to preview the 'Follow On' section before reading the stories with students.

Jane Leggett

TONI CADE BAMBARA

Raymond's Run

I don't have much work to do around the house like some girls. My mother does that. And I don't have to earn my pocket money by hustling; George runs errands for the big boys and sells Christmas cards. And anything else that's got to get done, my father does. All I have to do in life is mind my brother Raymond, which is enough.

Sometimes I slip and say my little brother Raymond. But as any fool can see he's much bigger and he's older too. But a lot of people call him my little brother cause he needs looking after cause he's not quite right. And a lot of smart mouths got lots to say about that too, especially when George was minding him. But now, if anybody has anything to say to Raymond, anything to say about his big head, they have to come by me. And I don't play the dozens or believe in standing around with somebody in my face doing a lot of talking. I much rather just knock you down and take my chances even if I am a little girl with skinny arms and a squeaky voice, which is how I got the name Squeaky. And if things get too rough, I run. And as anybody can tell you, I'm the fastest thing on two feet.

There is no track meet that I don't win the first place medal. I used to win the twenty-yard dash when I was a little kid in kindergarten. Nowadays, it's the fifty-yard dash. And tomorrow

I'm subject to run the quarter-metre relay all by myself and come in first, second, and third. The big kids call me Mercury cause I'm the swiftest thing in the neighbourhood. Everybody knows that – except two people who know better, my father and me. He can beat me to Amsterdam Avenue with me having a two fire-hydrant headstart and him running with his hands in his pockets and whistling. But that's private information. Cause can you imagine some thirty-five-year-old man stuffing himself into PAL shorts to race little kids? So as far as everyone's concerned, I'm the fastest and that goes for Gretchen, too, who has put out the tale that she is going to win the first-place medal this year. Ridiculous. In the second place, she's got short legs. In the third place, she's got freckles. In the first place, no one can beat me and that's all there is to it.

I'm standing on the corner admiring the weather and about to take a stroll down Broadway so I can practise my breathing exercises, and I've got Raymond walking on the inside close to the buildings, cause he's subject to fits of fantasy and starts thinking he's a circus performer and that the kerb is a tightrope strung high in the air. And sometimes after a rain he likes to step down off his tightrope right into the gutter and slosh around getting his shoes and cuffs wet. Then I get hit when I get home. Or sometimes if you don't watch him he'll dash across traffic to the island in the middle of Broadway and give the pigeons a fit. Then I have to go behind him apologising to all the old people sitting around trying to get some sun and getting all upset with the pigeons fluttering around them, scattering their newspapers and upsetting the waxpaper lunches in their laps. So I keep Raymond on the inside of me, and he plays like he's driving a stage coach which is OK by me so long as he doesn't run me over or interrupt my breathing exercises, which I have to do on account of I'm serious about my running, and I don't care who knows it.

Now some people like to act like things come easy to them, won't let on that they practise. Not me. I'll high-prance down 34th Street like a rodeo pony to keep my knees strong even if it does get my mother uptight so that she walks ahead like she's not with me, don't know me, is all by herself on a shopping trip, and I am somebody else's crazy child. Now you take Cynthia

Procter for instance. She's just the opposite. If there's a test tomorrow, she'll say something like, 'Oh, I guess I'll play handball this afternoon and watch television tonight,' just to let you know she ain't thinking about the test. Or like last week when she won the spelling bee for the millionth time, 'A good thing you got "receive", Squeaky, cause I would have got it wrong. I completely forgot about the spelling bee.' And she'll clutch the lace on her blouse like it was a narrow escape. Oh, brother. But of course when I pass her house on my early morning trots around the block, she is practising the scales on the piano over and over and over and over. Then in music class she always lets herself get bumped around so she falls accidentally on purpose onto the piano stool and is so surprised to find herself sitting there that she decides just for fun to try out the ole keys. And what do you know – Chopin's waltzes just spring out of her fingertips and she's the most surprised thing in the world. A regular prodigy. I could kill people like that. I stay up all night studying the words for the spelling bee. And you can see me any time of day practising running. I never walk if I can trot, and shame on Raymond if he can't keep up. But of course he does, cause if he hangs back someone's liable to walk up to him and get smart, or take his allowance from him, or ask him where he got that great big pumpkin head. People are so stupid sometimes.

So I'm strolling down Broadway breathing out and breathing in on counts of seven, which is my lucky number, and here comes Gretchen and her sidekicks: Mary Louise, who used to be a friend of mine when she first moved to Harlem from Baltimore and got beat up by everybody till I took up for her on account of her mother and my mother used to sing in the same choir when they were young girls, but people ain't grateful, so now she hangs out with the new girl Gretchen and talks about me like a dog; and Rosie, who is as fat as I am skinny and has a big mouth where Raymond is concerned and is too stupid to know that there is not a big deal of difference between herself and Raymond and that she can't afford to throw stones. So they are steady coming up Broadway and I see right away that it's going to be one of those Dodge City scenes cause the street ain't that big and they're close to the buildings just as we are. First I think I'll step into the candy store and look over the new comics and let them pass. But that's chicken and I've got a reputation to consider. So then I think I'll just walk straight on through them or even over them if necessary. But as they get to me, they slow down. I'm ready to fight, cause like I said I don't feature a whole lot of chit-chat, I much prefer to just knock you down right from the jump and save everybody a lotta precious time.

'You signing up for the May Day races?' smiles Mary Louise, only it's not a smile at all. A dumb question like that doesn't deserve an answer. Besides, there's just me and Gretchen standing there really, so no use wasting my breath talking to shadows.

'I don't think you're going to win this time,' says Rosie, trying to signify with her hands on her hips all salty, completely forgetting that I have whupped her behind many times for less salt than that.

'I always win cause I'm the best,' I say straight at Gretchen who is, as far as I'm concerned, the only one talking in this ventriloquist-dummy routine. Gretchen smiles, but it's not a smile, and I'm thinking that girls never really smile at each other because they don't know how and don't want to know how and there's probably no one to teach us how, cause grown-up girls don't know either. Then they all look at Raymond who has just brought his mule team to a standstill. And they're about to see what trouble they can get into through him.

'What grade you in now, Raymond?'

'You got anything to say to my brother, you say it to me, Mary Louise Williams of Raggedy Town, Baltimore.'

'What are you, his mother?' sasses Rosie.

'That's right, Fatso. And the next word out of anybody and I'll be *their* mother too.' So they just stand there and Gretchen shifts from one leg to the other and so do they. Then Gretchen puts her hands on her hips and is about to say something with her freckle-face self but doesn't. Then she walks around me looking me up and down but keeps walking up Broadway, and her sidekicks follow her. So me and Raymond smile at each other and he says, 'Gidyap' to his team and I continue with my breathing exercises, strolling down Broadway toward the ice man on 145th, with not a care in the world cause I am Miss Quicksilver herself.

I take my time getting to the park on May Day because the track meet is the last thing on the programme. The biggest thing on the programme is the May Pole dancing, which I can do without, thank you, even if my mother thinks it's a shame I don't take part and act like a girl for a change. You'd think my mother'd be grateful not to have to make me a white organdie dress with a big satin sash and buy me new white baby-doll shoes that can't be taken out of the box till the big day. You'd think she'd be glad her daughter ain't out there prancing around a May Pole getting the new clothes all dirty and sweaty and trying to act like a fairy or a flower or whatever you're supposed to be when you should be trying to be yourself, whatever that is, which is, as far as I am concerned, a poor Black girl who really can't afford to buy shoes and a new dress you only wear once a lifetime cause it won't fit next year.

I was once a strawberry in a Hansel and Gretel pageant when I was in nursery school and didn't have no better sense than to dance on tiptoe with my arms in a circle over my head doing umbrella steps and being a perfect fool just so my mother and father could come dressed up and clap. You'd think they'd know better than to encourage that kind of nonsense. I am not a strawberry. I do not dance on my toes. I run. That is what I am all about. So I always come late to the May Day programme, just in time to get my number pinned on and lay in the grass till they announce the fifty-yard dash.

I put Raymond in the little swings, which is a tight squeeze this year and will be impossible next year. Then I look around for Mr Pearson, who pins the numbers on. I'm really looking for Gretchen if you want to know the truth, but she's not around. The park is jam-packed. Parents in hats and corsages and breast-pocket handkerchiefs peeking up. Kids in white dresses and light-blue suits. The parkees unfolding chairs and chasing the rowdy kids from Lenox as if they had no right to be there. The big guys with their caps on backwards, leaning against the fence swirling the basketballs on the tips of their fingers, waiting for all these crazy people to clear out the park so they can play. Most of the kids in my class are carrying bass drums and glockenspiels and flutes. You'd think they'd put in a few bongos or something for real like that.

Then here comes Mr Pearson with his clipboard and his cards and pencils and whistles and safety pins and fifty million other things he's always dropping all over the place with his clumsy self. He sticks out in a crowd because he's on stilts. We used to call him Jack and the Beanstalk to get him mad. But I'm the only one that can outrun him and get away, and I'm too grown for that silliness now.

'Well, Squeaky,' he says, checking my name off the list and handing me number seven and two pins. And I'm thinking he's got no right to call me Squeaky, if I can't call him Beanstalk.

'Hazel Elizabeth Deborah Parker,' I correct him and tell him to write it down on his board.

'Well, Hazel Elizabeth Deborah Parker, going to give someone else a break this year?' I squint at him real hard to see if he is seriously thinking I should lose the race on purpose just to give someone else a break. 'Only six girls running this time,' he continues, shaking his head sadly like it's my fault all of New York didn't turn out in sneakers. 'That new girl should give you a run for your money.' He looks around the park for Gretchen like a periscope in a submarine movie. 'Wouldn't it be a nice gesture if you were . . . to ahh . . .'

I give him such a look he couldn't finish putting that idea into words. Grown-ups got a lot of nerve sometimes. I pin number seven to myself and stomp away, I'm so burnt. And I go straight for the track and stretch out on the grass while the band winds up with 'Oh, the Monkey Wrapped His Tail Around the Flag Pole,' which my teacher calls by some other name. The man on the loudspeaker is calling everyone over to the track and I'm on my back looking at the sky, trying to pretend I'm in the country, but I can't, because even grass in the city feels hard as sidewalk, and there's just no pretending you are anywhere but in a 'concrete jungle' as my grandfather says.

The twenty-yard dash takes all of two minutes cause most of the little kids don't know no better than to run off the track or run the wrong way or run smack into the fence and fall down and cry. One little kid, though, has got the good sense to run straight for the white ribbon up ahead so he wins. Then the second-graders line up for the thirty-yard dash and I don't even bother to turn my head to watch cause Raphael Perez always wins. He wins before he even begins by psyching the runners, telling them they're going to trip on their shoelaces and fall on their faces or lose their shorts or something, which he doesn't really have to do since he is very fast, almost as fast as I am. After that is the forty-yard dash which I use to run when I was in first grade. Raymond is hollering from the swings cause he knows I'm about to do my thing cause the man on the loud-speaker has just announced the fifty-yard dash, although he might just as well be giving a recipe for angel food cake cause you can hardly make out what he's sayin for the static. I get up and slip off my sweat pants and then I see Gretchen standing at the starting line, kicking her legs out like a pro. Then as I get into place I see that ole Raymond is on line on the other side of the fence, bending down with his fingers on the ground just like he knew what he was doing. I was going to yell at him but then I didn't. It burns up your energy to holler.

Every time, just before I take off in a race, I always feel like I'm in a dream, the kind of dream you have when you're sick with fever and feel all hot and weightless. I dream I'm flying over a sandy beach in the early morning sun, kissing the leaves of the trees as I fly by. And there's always the smell of apples, just like in the country when I was little and used to think I was a choo-choo train, running through the fields of corn and chugging up the hill to the orchard. And all the time I'm dreaming this, I get lighter and lighter until I'm flying over the beach again, getting blown through the sky like a feather that weighs nothing at all. But once I spread my fingers in the dirt and crouch over the Get on Your Mark, the dream goes and I am solid again and am telling myself, Squeaky you must win, you must win, you are the fastest thing in the world, you can even beat your father up Amsterdam if you really try. And then I feel my weight coming back just behind my knees then down to my feet then into the earth and the pistol shot explodes in my blood and I am off and weightless again, flying past the other runners, my arms pumping up and down and the whole world is quiet except for the crunch as I zoom over the gravel in the track. I glance to my left and there is no one. To the right, a blurred Gretchen, who's got her chin jutting out as if it would win the race all by itself. And on the other side of the fence is

Raymond with his arms down to his side and the palms tucked up behind him, running in his very own style, and it's the first time I ever saw that and I almost stop to watch my brother Raymond on his first run. But the white ribbon is bouncing toward me and I tear past it, racing into the distance till my feet with a mind of their own start digging up footfuls of dirt and brake me short. Then all the kids standing on the side pile on me, banging me on the back and slapping my head with their May Day programmes, for I have won again and everybody on 151st Street can walk tall for another year.

'In first place . . .' the man on the loudspeaker is clear as a bell now. But then he pauses and the loudspeaker starts to whine. Then static. And I lean down to catch my breath and here comes Gretchen walking back, for she's overshot the finish line too, huffing and puffing with her hands on her hips taking it slow, breathing in steady time like a real pro and I sort of like her a little for the first time. 'In first place . . .' and then three or four voices get all mixed up on the loudspeaker and I dig my sneaker into the grass and stare at Gretchen who's staring back, we both wondering just who did win. I can hear old Beanstalk arguing with the man on the loudspeaker and then a few others running their mouths about what the stopwatches say. Then I hear Raymond yanking at the fence to call me and I wave to shush him, but he keeps rattling the fence like a gorilla in a cage like in them gorilla movies, but then like a dancer or something he starts climbing up nice and easy but very fast. And it occurs to me, watching how smoothly he climbs hand over hand and remembering how he looked running with his arms down to his side and with the wind pulling his mouth back and his teeth showing and all, it occurred to me that Raymond would make a very fine runner. Doesn't he always keep up with me on my trots? And he surely knows how to breathe in counts of seven cause he's always doing it at the dinner table, which drives my brother George up the wall. And I'm smiling to beat the band cause if I've lost this race, or if me and Gretchen tied, or even if I've won, I can always retire as a runner and begin a whole new career as a coach with Raymond as my champion. After all, with a little more study I can beat Cynthia and her phony self at the spelling bee. And if I bugged my mother, I could get piano lessons and become a star. And I have a big rep as the baddest thing around. And I've got a roomful of ribbons and medals and awards. But what has Raymond got to call his own?

So I stand there with my new plans, laughing out loud by this time as Raymond jumps down from the fence and runs over with his teeth showing and his arms down to the side, which no one before him has quite mastered as a running style. And by the time he comes over I'm jumping up and down so glad to see him – my brother Raymond, a great runner in the family tradition. But of course everyone thinks I'm jumping up and down because the men on the loudspeaker have finally gotten themselves together and compared notes and are announcing 'In first place – Miss Hazel Elizabeth Deborah Parker.' (Dig that.) 'In second place – Miss Gretchen P. Lewis.' And I look over at Gretchen wondering what the 'P' stands for. And smile. Cause she's good, no doubt about it. Maybe she'd like to help me coach Raymond; she obviously is serious about running, as any fool can see. And she nods to congratulate me and then she smiles. And I smile. We stand there with this big smile of respect between us. It's about as real a smile as girls can do for each other, considering we don't practise real smiling every day, you know, cause maybe we too busy being flowers or fairies or strawberries instead of something honest and worthy of respect . . . you know . . . like being people!

DOROTHY M. JOHNSON

Flame on the Frontier

On Sunday morning, wearing white man's sober clothing, a Sioux chief named Little Crow attended the church service at the Lower Agency and afterwards shook hands with the preacher. On Sunday afternoon, Little Crow's painted and feathered Santee Sioux swooped down on the settlers in bloody massacre. There was no warning . . .

Hannah Harris spoke sharply to her older daughter, Mary Amanda. 'I've told you twice to get more butter from the spring. Now step! The men want to eat.'

The men – Oscar Harris and his two sons, sixteen and eighteen – sat in stolid patience on a bench in front of the cabin, waiting to be called to the table.

Mary Amanda put down the book she had borrowed from a distant neighbour and went unwillingly out of the cabin. She liked to read and was proud that she knew how, but she never had another book in her hands as long as she lived. Mary Amanda Harris was, on that day in August in 1862, just barely thirteen years old.

Her little sister Sarah tagged along down to the spring for lack of anything better to do. She was healthily hungry, and the smell of frying chicken had made her fidget until her mother had warned, 'Am I going to have to switch you?'

The two girls wrangled as they trotted down the accustomed path.

'Now what'd you come tagging for?' demanded Mary Amanda. She wanted to stay, undisturbed, in the world of the book she had been reading.

Sarah said, 'I guess I got a right to walk here as good as you.'

She shivered, not because of any premonition but simply because the air was cool in the brush by the spring. She glanced across the narrow creek and saw a paint-striped face. Before she could finish her scream, the Indian had leaped the creek and smothered her mouth.

At the cabin they heard that single, throat-tearing scream instantly muffled. They knew what had to be done; they had planned it, because this day might come to any frontier farm.

Hannah Harris scooped up the baby boy, Willie, and hesitated only to cry out, 'The girls?'

The father, already inside the cabin, handed one rifle to his eldest son as he took the other for himself. To Jim, who was sixteen, he barked, 'The axe, boy.'

Hannah knew what she had to do – run and hide – but that part of the plan had included the little girls, too. She was to take the four younger children, including the dull boy, Johnny. She was too sick with the meaning of that brief scream to be able to change the plan and go without the girls.

But Oscar roared, 'Run for the rushes! You crazy?' and broke her paralysis. With the baby under one arm she began to run down the hill to a place by the river where the rushes grew high.

The only reason Hannah was able to get to the rushes with her two youngest boys was that the men, Oscar and Jim and Zeke, delayed the Indians for a few minutes. The white men might have barricaded themselves in the cabin and stood off the attackers for a longer period, but the approaching Indians would have seen that frantic scuttling into the rushes.

Oscar and Jim and Zeke did not defend. They attacked. With the father going first, they ran towards the spring and met the Indians in the brush. Fighting there, they bought a little time for the three to hide down by the river, and they paid for it with their lives.

Hannah, the mother, chose another way of buying time. She

heard the invaders chopping at whatever they found in the cabin. She heard their howls as they found clothing and kettles and food. She stayed in the rushes as long as she dared, but when she smelled the smoke of the cabin burning, she knew the Indians would be ranging out to see what else might be found.

Then she thrust the baby into Johnny's arms, and said fiercely, 'You take care of him and don't you let him go until they kill you.'

She did not give him any instructions about how to get to a place of safety. There might be no such place.

She kissed Johnny on the forehead and she kissed the baby twice, because he was so helpless and because he was, blessedly, not crying.

She crawled to the left, far to the left of the children, so that she came dripping up out of the rushes and went shrieking up the hill straight towards the Indians.

When they started down to meet her, she hesitated and turned. She ran, still screaming, towards the river, as if she were so crazed she did not know what she was doing. But she knew. She knew very well. She did exactly what a meadowlark will do if its nest in the grass is menaced – she came into the open, crying and frantic, and lured the pursuit away from her young.

But the meadowlark acts by instinct, not by plan. Hannah Harris had to fight down her instinct, which was to try to save her own life.

As the harsh hands seized her, she threw her arm across her eyes so as not to see death . . .

Of the two girls down at the spring, only Sarah screamed. Mary Amanda did not have time. A club, swung easily by a strong arm, cracked against her head.

Sarah Harris heard the brief battle and knew her father's voice, but she did not have to see the bodies, a few yards away on the path, through the brush. One of the Indians held her without difficulty. She was a thin little girl, nine years old.

Mary Amanda was unconscious and would have drowned except that her guard pulled her out of the creek and laid her, face down, on the gravel bank.

The girls never saw their cabin again. Their captors tied their hands behind them and headed back the way they had come to rejoin the war party. The girls were too frightened to cry or speak. They stumbled through the brush.

Mary Amanda fell too many times. Finally she gave up and lay still, waiting to die, sobbing quietly. Her guard grunted and lifted his club.

Sarah flew at him shrieking. Her hands were tied, but her feet were free and she could still run.

'Don't you hurt my sister!' she scolded. 'Don't you do it, I say!' She bowed her head and butted him.

The Indian, who had never had anything to do with white people except at a distance, or in furious flurries of raiding, was astonished by her courage, and impressed. All he knew of white girls was that they ran away, screaming, and then were caught. This one had the desperate, savage fury of his own women. She chattered as angrily as a bluejay. (Bluejay was the name he gave her, the name everyone called her, in the years she lived and grew up among the Sioux.)

She had knocked the wind out of him, but he was amused. He jerked the older girl, Mary Amanda, to her feet.

The mother, Hannah, was taken along by the same route, about a mile behind them, but she did not know they were still alive. One of them she saw again six years later. The other girl she never saw again.

For hours she went stumbling, praying, 'Lord in thy mercy, make them kill me fast!'

When they did not, she let hope flicker, and when they camped that night, she began to ask timidly, 'God, could you help me get away?'

She had no food that night, and no water. An Indian had tied her securely.

The following day her captors caught up with a larger party, carrying much loot and driving three other white women. They were younger than Hannah. That was what saved her.

When she was an old woman, she told the tale grimly: 'I prayed to the Lord to let me go, and He turned the Indians' backs on me and I went into the woods, and that was how I got away.'

She did not tell how she would still hear the piercing shrieks of the other white women, even when she was far enough into the woods so that she dared to run.

She blundered through the woods, hiding at every sound, praying to find a trail, but terrified when she came to one, for fear there might be Indians around the next bend. After she reached the trail and began to follow it, she had a companion, a shaggy yellow dog.

For food during two days she had berries. Then she came upon the dog eating a grouse he had killed, and she stooped, but he growled.

'Nice doggie,' she crooned. 'Nice old Sheppy.'

She abased herself with such praise until – probably because he had caught other game and was not hungry – he let her take the tooth-torn, dirt-smeared remnants. She picked off the feathers with fumbling fingers, washed the raw meat in the creek and ate it as she walked.

She smelled wood smoke the next morning and crawled through brush until she could see a clearing. She saw white people there in front of a cabin, and much bustling. She heard children crying and the authoritative voices of women. She stood up then and ran, screaming, towards the cabin, with the dog jumping and barking beside her.

One of the hysterical women there seized a rifle and fired a shot at Hannah before a man shouted, 'She's white!' and ran out to meet her.

There were sixteen persons in the cramped cabin or near it – refugees from other farms. Hannah Harris kept demanding, while she wolfed down food, 'Ain't anybody seen two little girls? Ain't anybody seen a boy and a baby?'

Nobody had seen them.

The draggled-skirted women in the crowded cabin kept busy with their children, but Hannah Harris had no children any more – she who had had four sons and two daughters. She dodged among the refugees, beseeching, 'Can't I help with something? Ain't there anything I can do?'

A busy old woman said with sharp sympathy, 'Miz Harris, you go lay down some place. Git some sleep. All you been through.'

Hannah Harris understood that there was no room for her there. She stumbled outside and lay down in a grassy place in the shade. She slept, no longer hearing the squalling of babies and the wrangling of the women.

Hannah awoke to the crying of voices she knew and ran around to the front of the cabin. She saw two men carrying a stretcher made of two shirts buttoned around poles. A bundle sagged on the stretcher, and a woman was trying to lift it, but it cried with two voices.

Johnny lay there, clutching the baby, and both of them were screaming.

Kneeling, she saw blood on Johnny's feet and thought with horror, 'Did the Injuns do that?' Then she remembered, 'No, he was barefoot when we ran.'

He would not release the baby, even for her. He was gaunt, his ribs showed under his tattered shirt. His eyes were partly open, and his lips were drawn back from his teeth. He was only half conscious, but he still had strength enough to clutch his baby brother, though the baby screamed with hunger and fear.

Hannah said in a strong voice, 'Johnny, you can let go now. You can let Willie go. Johnny, this is your mother talking.'

With a moan, he let his arms go slack.

For the rest of his life, and he lived another fifty years, he suffered from nightmares, and often awoke screaming.

With two of her children there Hannah Harris was the equal of any woman. She pushed among the others to get to the food, to find cloth for Johnny's wounded feet. She wrangled with them, defending sleeping space for her children.

For a few months she made a home for her boys by keeping house for a widower named Lincoln Bartlett, whose two daughters had been killed at a neighbour's cabin. Then she married him.

The baby, Willie, did not live to grow up, in spite of the sacrifices that had been made for him. He died of diphtheria. While Link Bartlett dug a little grave, Hannah sat, stern but dry-eyed, on a slab bench, cradling the still body in her arms.

The dull boy, Johnny, burst out hoarsely, 'It wasn't no use after all, was it?' and his mother understood.

She told him strongly, 'Oh, yes, it was! It was worth while, all you did. He's dead now, but he died in my arms, with a roof over him. I'll know where he's buried. It ain't as if the Indians had butchered him some place that I'd never know.'

She carried the body across the room and laid it tenderly in the box that had been Willie's bed and would be his coffin. She turned to her other son and said, 'Johnny, come sit on my lap.'

He was a big boy, twelve years old, and he was puzzled by this invitation, as he was puzzled about so many things. Awkwardly he sat on her knees, and awkwardly he permitted her to cuddle his head against her shoulder.

'How long since your mother kissed you?' she asked, and he mumbled back, 'Don't know.'

She kissed his forehead. 'You're my big boy. You're my Johnny.'

He lay in her arms for a while, tense and puzzled. After a while, not knowing why it was necessary to cry, he began to sob, and she rocked him back and forth. She had no tears left.

Johnny said something then that he had thought over many times, often enough to be sure about it. 'It was him that mattered most, I guess.'

Hannah looked down at him, shocked.

'He was my child and I loved him,' she said. 'It was him I worried about . . . But it was you I trusted.'

The boy blinked and scowled. His mother bowed her head.

'I never said so. I thought you knowed that. When I give him to you that day, Johnny boy, I put more trust in you than I did in the Lord God.'

That was a thing he always remembered – the time his mother made him understand that for a while he had been more important than God.

The Harris sisters were sold twice, the second time to a Sioux warrior named Runs Buffalo, whose people ranged far to the westward.

Bluejay never had to face defeat among the Indians. The little girl who had earned her name by scolding angrily had the privileges of a baby girl. She was fed and cared for like the Indian children, and she had more freedom and less scolding than she had had in the cabin that was burned. Like the other little girls, she was freer than the boys. Her responsibility would not begin for three or four years. When the time came, she would be taught to do the slow, patient work of the women, in preparation for being a useful wife. But while she was little, she could play.

While the boys learned to shoot straight and follow tracks, while they tested and increased their endurance and strength, the little girls played and laughed in the sun. Bluejay did not even have a baby to look after, because she was the youngest child in the lodge of Runs Buffalo. She was the petted one, the darling, and the only punishment she knew was what she deserved for profaning holy objects. Once at home she had been switched by her father for putting a dish on the great family Bible. In the Indian village, she learned to avoid touching medicine bundles or sacred shields and to keep silent in the presence of men who understood religious mysteries.

Mary Amanda, stooped over a raw buffalo hide, scraping it hour after hour with tools of iron and bone, because that was the women's work and she was almost a woman, heard familiar shrill arguments among the younger girls, the same arguments that had sounded in the white settlement, and in the same language: 'You're it!' . . . 'I am not!'

That much the little Indian girls learned of English. Sarah learned Sioux so fast that she no longer needed English and would have stopped speaking it except that her older sister insisted.

Mary Amanda learned humility through blows. To her, everything about the Indians was contemptible. She learned their language simply to keep from being cuffed by the older women, who were less shocked at her ignorance of their skills than at her unwillingness to learn the work that was a woman's privilege to perform. She sickened at the business of softening hides with a mixture of clay and buffalo manure. If she had been more docile, she might have been an honoured daughter in the household. Instead, she was a sullen slave. Mary Amanda remembered what Sarah often forgot: that she was white. Mary Amanda never stopped hoping that they would be rescued. The name the Indians gave her was The Foreigner.

When she tried to take Sarah aside to talk English, the old woman of the household scolded.

Mary Amanda spoke humbly in Sioux. 'Bluejay forgets to

talk like our own people. I want her to know how to talk.'

The old woman growled, 'You are Indians,' and Mary Amanda answered, 'It is good for Indians to be able to talk to white people.'

The argument was sound. A woman interpreter would never be permitted in the councils of chiefs and captains, but who could tell when the skill might be useful? The girls were allowed to talk together, but Sarah preferred Sioux.

When The Foreigner was sixteen years old she had four suitors. She knew what a young man meant by sending a gift of meat to the lodge and later standing out in front, blanket-wrapped and silent.

When the young man came, Mary Amanda pretended not to notice, and the old woman pretended with her, but there was chuckling in the lodge as everyone waited to see whether The Foreigner would go out, perhaps to bring in water from the creek.

Her little sister teased her. 'Go on out. All you have to do is let him put his blanket around you and talk. Go on. Other girls do.'

'Indian girls do,' Mary Amanda answered sadly. 'That ain't the way boys do their courting back home.'

The tall young men were patient. Sometimes as many as three at once stood out there through twilight into darkness, silent and waiting. They were eligible, respected young men, skilled in hunting and taking horses, proved in courage, schooled in the mysteries of protective charms and chanted prayer. All of them had counted coup in battle.

Mary Amanda felt herself drawn towards the lodge opening. It would be so easy to go out!

She asked Sarah humbly, 'Do you think it's right, the way they buy their wives? Of course, the girl's folks give presents to pay back.'

Sarah shrugged. 'What other way is there? . . . If it was me, I'd go out fast enough. Just wait till I'm older!' She reminded her sister of something it was pleasanter to forget. 'They don't have to wait for you to make up your mind. They could sell you to an old man for a third wife.'

When Mary Amanda was seventeen, a man of forty, who had

an ageing wife, looked at her with favour, and she made her choice. On a sweet summer evening she arose from her place in the tepee and, without a word to anyone, stooped and passed through the lodge opening. She was trembling as she walked past Hawk and Grass Runner and eluded their reaching hands. She stopped before a young man named Snow Mountain.

He was as startled as the family back in the tepee. Courting The Foreigner had become almost a tradition with the young men, because she seemed unattainable and competition ruled their lives. He wrapped his blanket around her and felt her heart beating wildly.

He did not tell her she was pretty. He told her that he was brave and cunning. He told her he was a skilled hunter, his lodge never lacked for meat. He had many horses, most of them stolen from the Crows in quick, desperate raids.

Mary Amanda said, 'You give horses to buy what you want. Will Runs Buffalo give presents to you in return?'

That was terribly important to her. The exchange of gifts was in itself the ceremony. If she went to him with no dowry, she went without honour.

'I cannot ask about that,' he said. 'My mother's brother will ask.'

But Runs Buffalo refused.

'I will sell the white woman for horses,' he announced. 'She belongs to me. I paid for her.'

Mary Amanda went without ceremony, on a day in autumn, to the new lodge of Snow Mountain. She went without pride, without dowry. The lodge was new and fine, she had the tools and kettles she needed, and enough robes to keep the household warm. But all the household things were from his people, not hers. When she cried, he comforted her.

For her there was no long honeymoon of lazy bliss. Her conscience made her keep working to pay Snow Mountain for the gifts no one had given him. But she was no longer a slave, she was queen in her own household. An old woman, a relative of his mother, lived with them to do heavy work. Snow Mountain's youngest brother lived with him, helping to hunt and butcher and learning the skills a man needed to know.

Mary Amanda was a contented bride – except when she

remembered that she had not been born an Indian. And there was always in her mind the knowledge that many warriors had two wives, and that often the two wives were sisters.

'You work too hard,' Snow Mountain told her. 'Your little sister does not work hard enough.'

'She is young,' The Foreigner reminded him, feeling that she should apologise for Bluejay's shortcomings.

Snow Mountain said, 'When she is older, maybe she will come here.'

Afterwards she knew he meant that in kindness. But thinking of Sarah as her rival in the tepee, as her sister-wife, froze Mary Amanda's heart. She answered only, 'Bluejay is young.'

Sarah Harris, known as Bluejay, already had two suitors when she was only fourteen. One of them was only two or three years older than she was, and not suitable for a husband; he had few war honours and was not very much respected by anyone except his own parents. The other was a grown man, a young warrior named Horse Ears, very suitable and, in fact, better than the flighty girl had any right to expect.

When Sarah visited in her sister's lodge, she boasted of the two young men.

Mary Amanda cried out, 'Oh, no! You're too young to take a man. You could wait two years yet, maybe three. Sarah, some day you will go back home.'

Two years after the massacre, the first rumour that the Harris girls were alive reached the settlement, but it was nothing their mother could put much faith in. The rumour came in a round-about way, to Link Bartlett, Hannah's second husband, from a soldier at the fort, who had it from another solider, who had it from a white trader, who heard it from a Cheyenne. And all they heard was that two white sisters were with a Sioux village far to the westward. Rumours like that drifted in constantly. Two hundred women had been missing after that raid.

Two more years passed before they could be fairly sure that there were really two white sisters out there and that they were probably the Harrises.

After still another year, the major who commanded the army post nearest the settlement was himself convinced, and negotiations began for their ransom.

Link Bartlett raised every cent he could – he sold some of his best land – to buy the gifts for that ransom.

In the sixth year of the captivity, a cavalry detachment was ordered out on a delicate diplomatic mission – to find and buy the girls back, if possible.

Link Bartlett had his own horse saddled and was ready to leave the cabin, to go with the soldiers, when Hannah cried harshly, 'Link, don't you go! Don't you go away and leave me and the kids!'

The children were dull Johnny and a two-year-old boy, named Lincoln, after his father, the last child Hannah ever had.

Link tried to calm her. 'Now, Hannah, you know we planned I should go along to see they got back all right – if we can find 'em at all.'

'I ain't letting you go,' she said, 'If them soldiers can't make out without you, they're a poor lot.' Then she jarred him to his heels. She said, almost gently, 'Link, if I was to lose you, I'd die.'

That was the only time she ever hinted that she loved him. He never asked for any more assurance. He stayed at home because she wanted him there.

Mary Amanda's son was half a year old when the girls first learned there was hope of their being ransomed.

The camp crier, walking among the lodges, wailed out the day's news so that everyone in the village would know what was planned: 'Women, stay in the camp. Keep your children close to you where they will be safe. There is danger. Some white soldiers are camped on the other side of the hills. Three men will go out and talk to them. The three men are Runs Buffalo, Big Moon and Snow Mountain.'

Mary Amanda did not dare ask Snow Mountain anything. She watched him ride out with the other men, and then she sat on the ground in front of his tepee, nursing her baby. Bluejay came to the lodge and the two girls sat together in silence as the hours passed.

The men from the Sioux camp did not come back until three days later. When Snow Mountain was ready to talk, he remarked, 'The white soldiers came to find out about two white girls. They will bring presents to pay if the white girls want to go back.'

Mary Amanda answered, 'O-o-oh,' in a sigh like a frail breeze in prairie grass.

There was no emotion in his dark, stern face. He looked at her for a long moment, and at the baby. Then he turned away without explanation. She called after him, but he did not answer. She felt the dark eyes staring, heard the low voices. She was a stranger again, as she had not been for a long time.

Nothing definite had been decided at the parley with the white soldiers, the girls learned. The soldiers would come back sometime, bringing presents for ransom, and if the presents were fine enough, there would be talk and perhaps a bargain. Mary Amanda felt suddenly the need to prepare Sarah for life in the settlement. She told her everything she could remember that might be useful.

'You'll cook over a fire in a fireplace,' she said, 'and sew with thread, and you'll have to learn to knit.'

Bluejay whimpered, 'I wish you could come, too.'

'He wouldn't let me go, of course,' Mary Amanda answered complacently. 'He wouldn't let me take the baby, and I wouldn't leave without *him*. You tell them I got a good man. Be sure to tell them that.'

At night, remembering the lost heaven of the burned cabin, remembering the life that was far away and long ago, she cried a little. But she did not even consider begging Snow Mountain to let her go. She had offended him, but when he stopped brooding they would talk again. He had not said anything to her since he had tested her by telling her the ransom had been offered.

He did not even tell her that he was going away. He gave orders to the old woman in the lodge and discussed plans with his younger brother, but he ignored his wife. Five men were going out to take horses from the Crows, he said. Mary Amanda shivered.

Before he rode away with his war party, he spent some time playing with the baby, bouncing the child on his knee, laughing when the baby laughed. But he said nothing to Mary Amanda, and the whole village knew that he was angry and that she deserved his anger.

Her hands and feet were cold as she watched him go, and her heart was gnawed by the fear that was part of every Indian woman's life: 'Maybe he will never come back.'

Not until the white soldiers had come back to parley again did she understand how cruelly she had hurt him.

She dreamed of home while they waited for news of the parley, and she tried to make Bluejay dream of it.

'You'll have to do some things different there, but Ma will remind you. I'll bet Ma will cry like everything when she sees you coming.' Mary Amanda's eyes flooded with tears, seeing that meeting. 'I don't remember she ever did cry,' she added thoughtfully, 'but I guess she must have sometimes . . . Ma must have got out of it all right. Who else would be sending the ransom? Oh, well, sometimes I'll find out all about it from Snow Mountain . . . I wonder if she got Johnny and Willie away from the cabin safe. Tell her I talked about her lots. Be sure to tell Ma that, Sarah. Tell her how cute my baby is.'

Bluejay, unnaturally silent, dreamed with her, wide-eyed, of the reunion, the half-forgotten heaven of the settlement.

'Tell her about Snow Mountain,' Mary Amanda reminded her sister. 'Be sure to do that. How he's a good hunter, so we have everything we want, and more. And everybody respects him. Tell her he's good to me and the baby . . . But Sarah, don't ever say he steals horses. They wouldn't understand, back home . . . And don't ever let on a word about scalps. If they say anything about scalps, you say our people here don't do that.'

'They do, though,' Sarah reminded her flatly. 'It takes a brave man to stop and take a scalp off when somebody's trying to kill him.'

Looking at her, Mary Amanda realised that Sarah didn't even think taking scalps was bad, so long as your own people did it and didn't have it done to them.

'You're going to have to forget some things,' she warned with a sigh.

While the parley was still on, Big Moon, the medicine priest, came to the lodge where The Foreigner bent over her endless work. He was carrying something wrapped in buckskin.

'Tell them the names of the people in your lodge before you came to the Sioux,' he said shortly as he put down the buckskin bundle. 'They are not sure you are the women they want.'

In the bundle were sheets of paper and a black crayon.

Sarah came running. She sat fascinated as Mary Amanda wrote carefully on the paper: 'Popa, Moma, Zeke, Jim, Johny, Wily.'

Mary Amanda was breathless when she finished. She squeezed Sarah's arm. 'Just think, you're going to go home!'

Sarah nodded, not speaking. Sarah was getting scared.

The following day, the ransom was paid and brought into camp. Then The Foreigner learned how much she had offended Snow Mountain.

Big Moon brought fine gifts to the lodge, and piled them inside – a gun, powder and percussion caps and bullets, bolts of cloth, mirrors and beads and tools and a copper kettle.

'The Foreigner can go now,' he said.

Mary Amanda stared. 'I cannot go back to the white people. I am Snow Mountain's woman. This is his baby.'

'The gifts pay also for the baby,' Big Moon growled. 'Snow Mountain will have another wife, more sons. He does not need The Foreigner. He has sold her to the white man.'

Mary Amanda turned pale. 'I will not go with the white men,' she said angrily. 'When Snow Mountain comes back, he will see how much The Foreigner's people cared for her. They have sent these gifts as her dowry.'

Big Moon scowled. 'Snow Mountain may not come back. He had a dream, and the dream was bad. His heart is sick, and he does not want to come back.'

As a widow in the Sioux camp, her situation would be serious. She could not go back to her parents' home, for she had no parents. But neither could she leave the camp now to go back to the settlement and never know whether Snow Mountain was alive or dead. Sarah stood staring at her in horror.

'I will wait for him,' Mary Amanda said, choking. 'Will Big Moon pray and make medicine for him?'

The fierce old man stared at her, scowling. He knew courage when he saw it, and he admired one who dared to gamble for high stakes.

'All these gifts will belong to Big Moon,' she promised, 'if Snow Mountain comes back.'

The medicine priest nodded and turned away. 'Bluejay must come with me,' he said briefly. 'I will take her to the white soldiers and tell them The Foreigner does not want to come.'

She watched Sarah walk away between the lodges after the medicine priest. She waved good-bye, and then went into the lodge. The old woman said, 'Snow Mountain has a good wife . . .'

Ten days passed before the war party came back. Mary Amanda waited, hardly breathing, as they brought Snow Mountain into camp tied on a travois, a pony drag.

Big Moon said, 'His shadow is gone out of his body. I do not know whether it will come back to stay.'

'I think it will come back to stay,' said The Foreigner, 'because I have prayed and made a sacrifice.'

At the sound of her voice, Snow Mountain opened his eyes. He lay quiet in his pain, staring up at her, not believing. She saw tears on his dark cheeks.

Her name was always The Foreigner, but for the rest of her life she was a woman of the Santee Sioux.

Sarah Harris, who had been called Bluejay, was hard to tame, they said in the settlement. Her mother fretted over her heathen ways. The girl could not even make bread!

'I can tan hides,' Sarah claimed angrily. 'I can butcher a buffalo and make pemmican. I can pitch a tepee and pack it on a horse to move.'

But those skills were not valued in a white woman, and Sarah found the settlement not quite heaven. She missed the constant talk and laughter of the close-pitched tepees. She had to learn a whole new system of polite behaviour. There was dickering and trading and bargaining, instead of a proud exchange of fine gifts. A neighbour boy slouching on a bench outside the cabin, talking to her stepfather while he got up courage to ask whether Sarah was at home, was less flattering as a suitor than a young warrior, painted and feathered, showing off on a spotted horse. Sometimes Sarah felt that she had left heaven behind her.

But she never went back to it. When she was seventeen, she married the blacksmith, Herman Schwartz, and their first baby was born six months later.

Sarah's child was six and her second child was three when the Indian man appeared at the door of her cabin and stood silently peering in.

'Git out of here!' she cried, seizing the broom.

He answered in the Sioux tongue, 'Bluejay has forgotten.'

She gave Horse Ears a shrill welcome in his own language and the three-year-old started to cry. She lifted a hand for an accustomed slap but let it fall. Indian mothers did not slap their children.

But she was not Indian any more, she recollected. She welcomed Horse Ears in as a white woman does an invited guest. In her Sunday-company voice she chatted politely. It was her privilege because she was a white woman. No need any more for the meek silence of the Indian woman.

She brought out bread and butter and ate with him. That was her privilege, too.

'My sister?' she asked.

He had not seen The Foreigner for a long time. He had left that village.

'Does Bluejay's man make much meat?' Horse Ears asked. 'Is he a man with many honours in war?'

She laughed shrilly. 'He makes much meat. He has counted coup many times. We are rich.'

'I came to find out those things,' he answered. 'In my lodge there is only one woman.'

She understood, and her heart leaped with the flattery. He had travelled far, and in some danger, to find out that all was well with her. If it was not, there was refuge in his tepee. And not only now, she realised, but any time, forever.

A shadow fell across the threshold; a hoarse voice filled the room. 'What's that bloody Injun doing here?' roared Sarah's husband. 'Are you all right?'

'Sure, we're all right,' she answered. 'I don't know who he is. He was hungry.'

His eyes narrowed with anger. 'Is he one of them you used to know?'

Her body tensed with fear. 'I don't know him, I told you!'

Her husband spoke to the Indian in halting Sioux, but Horse Ears was wise. He did not answer.

'Git out!' the blacksmith ordered, and the Indian obeyed without a word.

As Sarah watched him go down the path, without turning, she wished fervently that she could tell him good-bye, could thank him for coming. But she could not betray him by speaking.

Herman Schwartz strode towards her in silent, awesome, blazing fury. She did not cringe; she braced her body against the table. He gave her a blow across the face that rocked her and blinded her.

She picked up the heavy iron skillet.

'Don't you ever do that again or I'll kill you,' she warned.

He glared at her with fierce pride, knowing that she meant what she said.

'I don't reckon I'll have to do it again,' he said complacently. 'If I ever set eyes on that savage again, I'll kill him. You know that, don't you, you damn squaw?'

She shrugged. 'Talk's cheap.'

As she went down to the spring for a bucket of water, she was singing.

Her girlhood was gone, and her freedom was far behind her. She had two crying children and was pregnant again. But two men loved her, and both of them had just proved it.

Forty years later, her third child was elected to the state legislature, and she went, a frightened, white-haired widow, to see him there. She was proud, but never so proud as she had been on a summer day three months before he was born.

STELLA IBEKWE

The Ugliest of Them All

She was the ugliest creature I had ever laid eyes on. I wouldn't have minded, but she just wouldn't change for the better. She tried to wear different cosmetics to look nice; it didn't work so she insisted on staying with me, to spoil my image too.

She was silent and would only speak when I spoke. She did everything I did, and worst of all, she always chose to wear the same clothes as me. She was with me everywhere I went, to school, church, discos and parties.

Even when we were apart, she still seemed to haunt me. She was a trespasser on my conscience, and she often turned my dreams into nightmares. One night, with a wicked smile on her ugly face, she told me in my dream that I had to either love or hate her.

By morning, my mind was made up. I looked into the mirror, and told her how much I hated her.

ADÈLE GERAS

Snapshots of Paradise

'You some kind of a cousin or something, is that right?' Gene lay on his back on the grass and looked at Fran.

'I suppose I am,' she said. 'I don't think I know the proper name for it. My great-grandmother and Grandma Sarah were sisters.'

'How come she ran all the way over there to England, then? Whyn't she stay here?'

Fran considered. Finally: 'She never said. But she never really became English, you know. Even after all the years. She still felt she belonged here.' Fran waved her hand to include not only the garden and the white frame house behind them, but the road and the apple orchard, the county, the state and the crazy quilting of all the other states: coast to coast, mountain and river, shanty and skyscraper – her great-grandmother's beloved U.S. of A.

'Betcha nearly took a fit when you heard what she'd left you in her will,' Gene chuckled.

'She wasn't a rich woman,' Fran said. 'She didn't leave much. I think an airline ticket is a very good thing to leave someone.'

'You saying you couldn't have made it over here without her help?' Being poor was not something Gene could easily imagine, Fran knew. She felt a desire to punch her newly discovered

35

cousin or whatever he was right on his freckled nose. Spoilt brat! But:

'No, I couldn't,' she answered shortly. After all, she reminded herself, you are a guest in this house.

'Well, you sure picked yourself a fine time,' said Gene. 'Sixtieth wedding anniversary and all.' He nodded at the grown-ups clustering under a huge elm tree. 'I don't know why they have to get Ma Jenkins to take the photo. Family group, they call it, like it was something special. I could've done it.'

'But then you wouldn't have been in it.'

'What about Harry? What're they going to do about him?'

'Patti said they'd bring him down in his wheelchair.'

Gene rolled over on the grass, doubled up with laughter. 'Hey, that's terrific. That's just about going to kill Harry off, you know what I mean? Can't you just see it? A photograph on someone's table or something for ever and ever, and who's the one in a wheelchair? Grandpa, who's eighty-four? No? Then Grandma Sarah perhaps, who still looks like she could shimmy all night? Maybe Joe, or Patti, or one of the aunts? Maybe Jean, who's always looked half dead? Oh, no sirree, that there's Harry in the wheelchair . . . Remember him? Track champion? Cheerleaders' darling? Golden Boy? Superman of 1983 and all the years before that? Isn't that peachy? Just terrific. He's sure gonna love you for that, honey.'

'Me?' Fran said. 'Why me? I didn't have anything to do with the crash. That happened weeks ago, before I even got here. Why should he blame me?'

'Won't blame you for the crash, kiddo. Blame you for the snapshot.'

'But why? It wasn't even my idea, this family group. I think it was your mother . . .'

'But you're the cousin specially over here visiting all the way from England . . . stands to reason you've got to have a shot of the family, right? Besides, it's your camera.'

Fran was silent. She glanced towards the house. Sure enough, Eleanor – Gene's and Harry's mother – was pushing a wheelchair across the grass. Harry's hair fell over his brow, shadowing his eyes.

'Why did you call him a Golden Boy?' she asked Gene. 'His

hair is dark. Almost black. You're more golden than he is.'

'Boy, are you dumb!' Gene sat up. 'Goldenness doesn't have one single thing to do with hair. Golden, that's the kind of person you are – successful, handsome, smart – you get what I mean. It's up here.' He tapped his skull and laughed. 'I'm about as golden as a pair of sneakers with holes in them. Listen to it: you can't hear what they're saying, but I'll tell you: Harry, how's it? How's it going, kid? Won't be long before you're back in training. Are you too hot? Too cold? Is everything OK? Would you like to sit here? Or over there, honey? Is the sun in your eyes? . . . move that wheelchair a little bit, Eleanor . . . I could go on and on.'

'He's been injured,' said Fran. 'It's only natural that they should make a fuss over him. I think you're just plain jealous.'

'I guess,' Gene said. 'I guess I am. It's the natural condition for an Ugly Duckling born a brother to the swanniest swan of the lot.'

'And look what happened to the Ugly Duckling, Gene,' said Fran. 'Anyway, you're not one. Not really. Your nose is out of joint, that's all.'

'Well,' Gene sighed. 'I should be used to it by now. I've lived with it for sixteen years. Ain't nothing new to me.'

Joe, Gene's grandfather, hurried towards them. From a distance, with his crew-cut hair and military style shirt, he looked like a young man.

'C'mon, you kids. Time to get lined up now.' Gene and Fran scrambled to their feet and walked over to where the others were in the process of sorting themselves out. Patti, Joe's wife and Gene's and Harry's grandmother seemed to be in charge of organising the group.

'OK now. We've got Grandma Sarah and Grandpa right in the middle. Leave a space there behind them for Joe and me . . . right? Then I guess . . . yeah, Susan, Rose and Jean, can you kind of group yourselves around Grandma Sarah? Right, that's great . . . where's that husband of yours, Rose? Oh! OK, Bill, I've got you now. Whyn't you come over and stand by Grandpa? That's just fine. Eleanor, you still count as one of the younger generation, come on down here now, near the front . . . and you kids, right on the bottom row. Let's put Franny between the

boys, OK? Kneel down, that's it. Cross-legged would be even
better. Great. We've got it. Now don't move a muscle, anyone.
I'll just race around to the back, then you can go ahead and
press that button.' Patti tottered across the grass in high-heeled
sandals. Ma Jenkins, an unsuspecting neighbour who'd only
called in on her way to church to wish the old folks a happy
anniversary, came forward hesitantly. 'Lordy, what a responsibility! Is this right? Do I have to focus it? Is this the right
button? Gee, I'll feel just terrible if it doesn't come out . . .'

She pressed the button. The photograph slid out of the
bottom of the camera. The family group broke up and gathered
round Ma Jenkins to watch the ghostly shapes sharpen, to
watch the colours brighten. 'Just plain old magic, that's what it
is,' said Ma Jenkins as she handed the camera back to Fran,
relieved that her part in the adventure was over.

10:00 a.m. FAMILY GROUP
Grandma Sarah looks pretty in a lace blouse, not much
different from the way she looked back in the 1920's when
she used to Charleston all night in beaded dresses. She has
been married for sixty years to the same man: Grandpa, who
used to be a snappy dresser and now wears a beach shirt with
palm trees printed on it. Patti has on a shirtwaist dress and
wears her hair in bangs. She looks like an older version of
Doris Day. The three weird sisters, as Gene has liked to call
them ever since he read Macbeth in high school, don't look
like sisters at all – not to each other and not to upstanding,
military Joe, who is their brother. Susan is the plump and
homely one. She has harlequin glasses and a big smile. Rose is
the skinny, glamorous one, gold bangles and heavy rings
weighing down her hands. Bill, her husband, is half-hidden
behind Joe. That's typical. Jean looks like an old lady, al-
though she's younger than all of them. It's the hair in a bun,
the brooch at the collar of a plain white blouse. It's the eyes.
Grandma Sarah has eyes with more youth in them. Eleanor
looks like a sister to her sons. Her long, reddish hair falls over
her face. Her skirt is pink cotton, Mexican, embroidered with
flowers and birds in fire colours. Fran, Gene and Harry are at
the front. Fran is wearing jeans and a T-shirt, looking quite

American for a beginner. Gene is looking at her. She is looking at Harry. And Harry is looking straight at the camera.

I suppose, Fran had thought when she first saw the swimming-pool, that this is what they mean by Culture Shock. A week of being in the United States still hadn't accustomed her to the idea that ordinary people (well, quite wealthy, OK, but not disgustingly, stinkingly rich) had such things right in their back garden. She spent a lot of time there, partly because she liked swimming, partly because it was so hot and partly to talk to Harry. Mostly, perhaps, to talk to Harry. Ever since the crash, he had made a kind of den for himself down by the pool, under an umbrella, with a table next to him, and all the comforts of his room around him, it seemed. Gene had rigged up a portable TV; he had a radio; there were books – anything he could possibly want. Fran felt newly shy each day as she approached him. She felt she was invading his privacy. And today? Would he be angry with her about the photograph? He didn't look angry. He was smiling.

'Hey, Fran,' he called as he saw her coming down the steps from the house, 'come on over and talk to me. I'm going crazy in all this heat with no one to talk to.'

'Sure,' Fran said and sat down beside him. 'What do you want to talk about today?'

'I dunno. Life, love, art, death, the usual stuff. You liking it here?'

'It's wonderful. I mean it.' Fran laughed. 'I never thought it'd be anything like this.'

' "Paradise for Kids" my grandmother calls it. Gene and me, we always call it that, and I guess it was a kind of Paradise when we were kids . . . but now, we say it kind of sarcastically, know what I mean? I mean the joint round here is not exactly jumping . . .'

'Do you miss the city? Is that it?'

'I guess . . . my friends, more than anything. And there's nothing to do except talk to your own family . . . that's why I like talking to you. You're different.'

Fran blushed. 'Different . . . is that good or bad?'

'It's good. I like it. I like hearing about England and the stuff you do back there. And I can tell you things. You're family and not family at the same time . . . d'you know what I mean?'

'May I ask you something then?' Fran said.

'Sure . . . anything you like . . .'

'Tell me about your father. No one ever mentions him.'

Harry frowned and said nothing for a moment. Fran looked at him: the smooth brown line of his neck, his straight nose, the toes sticking out of the plaster casts he wore on both legs, and felt as though some part of her, some inner substance of which she was unaware, were dissolving, melting in the warmth of the love she was feeling. She identified it as love at that moment, while she was waiting for Harry to speak. She hadn't thought of it by a name before, only that she liked to look at him, liked the sound his voice made, waited for him to come into a room if he were absent, thought of him, imagined . . . Now that she had given it a name, Fran felt both anguish and relief. Relief, because it's always a comfort to know the actual name of the disease you're suffering from, and anguish because in five days she would be back in England and Harry would be here, and that would be that.

But, said a tiny, hopeful voice from somewhere inside her head, what if he loved you? Really loved you? He could visit . . . you could visit . . . you could marry . . . have kids . . . Paradise for kids . . . live in Paradise . . .

Another voice, stronger, harder, so much more sensible, also inside her head: 'Don't be a bloody fool. Why should he? Love you? Look at you? Kiss you? Want to marry you, for Heaven's sake. Are you nuts? A face like that? A body like that? A Golden Boy? Forget it.'

Fran could picture Harry's future with a certainty that muffled her heart and made her catch her breath: Mr and Mrs Golden, right here in Paradise, a modern equivalent of Grandpa and Grandma Sarah. Almost, she could imagine Harry's sixtieth wedding anniversary. Forget it, she thought. Take it out at night, this love, and look at it for a while before sleeping. Keep the 'what ifs' and the 'maybes' for the dark hours. Don't let this love out into the open.

'Aren't you listening to me, Fran?' Harry said.

'Of course I am, Harry, go on.'

'Well, like I said, he hurt my mom a lot. Just taking off like that without a word to anyone. I was six. Gene was four. I don't like to remember that time. I don't like to talk about it. Later on, there was the divorce and stuff like that, and that was tough, but the worst was at the beginning. Every day I'd get back from school and think: he'll be back today, for sure. Today will be the day. But it never was.'

'That's dreadful. I don't know what to say.'

'That's OK. We'll talk about something else. I'll tell you a secret if you like.'

'A secret? Great!' Fran smiled.

'But first you've got to turn me over, OK? Can you do that, being so little and all?'

'Of course I can. I'm little but tough.' Fran wondered how the words came out at all, what with the rush of feeling that seemed to fill her throat.

'Right,' said Harry. 'You put both arms round my waist and kind of twist and I'll lever myself round with my arms. OK?'

Fran nodded. She put both arms around his waist and turned him towards her. His skin was warm from the sun and he smelled – like what? Air, and water and light and sweat and suntan oil and soap.

'There you go,' she said as she pulled him round. She took her hands away as soon as she could and hugged herself to stop the trembling.

'You're not through yet, kid,' Harry said. 'Slavedriver Harry requires that you oil his back.'

'OK,' said Fran as lightly as she could. 'Where's the oil?'

'Right there.'

Fran rubbed oil into Harry's back, moving her hands in long, smooth strokes. She felt drunk: silence filled her ears, a mist of heat seemed to hang over the house, over the pool. Time didn't exist any more. The whole universe had gathered itself up into these movements, this feeling, Harry's skin under her hands. She felt hypnotised, dazed, she couldn't bring her hands to stop and then . . . (how did it happen? Later, she would try and reconstruct the exact series of movements, try to slow them and slow them and play them back in her mind, like a video, frame by frame) . . . there was a hand behind her head and her mouth was suddenly on Harry's and she was breathing him in, tasting him, smelling the suntan oil, and his hair and then it was over. Fran could think of nothing to say. She looked at the pool, at the house, anywhere but at Harry.

'You're a cute kid, you know that?'

Fran struggled, started to speak and couldn't. She coughed and stood up. In her embarrassment, she put on a false American accent:

'Gee, t'anks!' she said. 'I've got to go now. I want to get a picture of the house, from the front . . . I'll see you later.'

'What about the secret?' Harry called after her. 'Don't you want to hear it?'

Fran had forgotten all about it, and right now didn't much care if she heard it or not. All she wanted to do was get away by herself somewhere and relive that kiss – the further away the better, but:

'Yes, of course I do. Tell.'

'It's Gene,' Harry said. 'He's nuts about you. Honestly.'

'That's rubbish!' Fran laughed. 'It can't be true, and even if it were true, he'd never tell you.'

'He doesn't have to,' said Harry. 'I'm his brother, remember? I can read his mind.'

Could it be true? Fran felt hot and confused. She had to think. Whatever was she to do now? If Gene loved her, and she loved Harry, and Harry loved . . . but who did Harry love? Her? Or was it just a friendly, cousinly kiss? It didn't feel like it. It felt like the real thing, although Fran admitted to herself that she hadn't had enough kisses to be able to spot any differences there might be between them. She shook her head. A person could develop a headache from thinking such thoughts in this heat.

'I'm going to get a shot of the front of the house,' she said. 'See you, Harry.'

'OK,' said Harry, and waved to her as he turned to his book.

11:30 a.m. THE HOUSE. LONG SHOT
A large white house set on a grassy slope. Plants grow over the railings of the front porch. There's a row of windows above the porch, and another two windows above that, under the gabled roof. To the right of the house is Grandma Sarah's

rose garden. She's been working on it since 1930 and is 'just about getting it into shape'. She still works on it, when she feels good. Just visible behind the house: a corner of the pool. It looks like a chip of aquamarine lying on green velvet.

Fran was in the kitchen, whipping cream for the strawberry shortcake: Grandpa's favourite and the final touch to a meal that seemed to have been in preparation for days. Susan, Rose and Jean had undertaken to put it together, but it looked to Fran as if Jean were doing most of the work, and the others were just gossiping: to each other and to her. Susan said: 'If Mike had lived, it would have been our thirty-fifth wedding anniversary this year.' She sighed as she licked a spoon. 'Did I tell you how we met? My sisters laugh at me, honey, but I reckon it's the most romantic thing. Mike rang up my boss, see, for something or other one day, and I answered the 'phone, of course, being his secretary.

'And he didn't say a thing to me, but when he'd finished his business with my boss, he said –'

' "Tell that secretary of yours that she's the woman I'm going to marry!" ' chorused Rose and Jean, and started laughing.

'Gee, Sue,' Rose said, 'I wish I had a dollar for each time you told that story!'

Jean just shook her head. Susan looked thwarted, sulky, like a small child. She turned to Fran.

'Don't pay them no mind, they're just jealous. Nothing that romantic ever happened to them, is all.'

Rose smiled slyly and began arranging plump strawberries on eiderdowns of fluffy cream. 'You saying my Bill isn't romantic, Sue? Well, I guess you're right at that. He isn't. But he's steady. There's a lot to be said for reliability. Even predictability. I know where I am with Bill . . .'

Jean, with her back to her sisters, took the empty cream bowl from Fran and winked at her and whispered, 'Dullsville . . . that's where she is with Bill. And she knows it, too.'

'I hear you whispering there,' Sue cried. 'Little Jeannie with the light brown hair! What're you whispering about?'

'Fran's telling me all her secrets,' said Jean.

'No, I wasn't –' Fran began.

'She's kidding,' said Rose. 'Jean always kids everyone. We reckon that's why she never married. Never did seem to take anyone seriously. Don't let the way she dresses fool you, Fran. Not for a minute. That's just a front . . .'

'Rose! Just because you spend your days all gussied up, doesn't mean that everyone . . .'

'Cut it out, will you?' Sue, the eldest sister, placed small rosebuds round the cake. It occurred to Fran that she had probably been saying the same thing to Rose and Jean for half a century. 'You're behaving like a couple of kids . . . bickering . . .'

'Who's bickering?' said Patti, coming into the kitchen. 'Why, that is a cake of cakes! Wait till they see that. Seems almost too good to eat. Maybe Fran can take a photograph of it, so that we never forget it. What do you say, Fran?'

'Yes,' said Fran, 'only I want you, too. All of you. Could you stand behind the cake?'

'Right,' said Patti. 'Shall I sit right here, behind it?' She smiled as her sisters-in-law gathered around her. Fran took the photograph.

2:00 p.m. THE KITCHEN. PATTI, SUSAN, ROSE, JEAN,
AND THE STRAWBERRY SHORTCAKE
On the whorls and lines of the scrubbed pine table, a blue plate holding a skyscraper of a cake: four golden shortcake circles, four snowdrifts of cream, strawberries like spots of blood just visible. Around the base of the cake, pink rosebuds and green leaves. At the other end of the table, Patti sits, and her husband's sisters lean over her shoulders and put their faces near hers so that the eye of the camera can see them all, catch them all, laughing. Happy that the cake has turned out so well. Sixty years married to the same person calls for a cake like this, their eyes say. Patti and Joe will perhaps live to deserve this kind of a cake, but it's too late for Susan and Jean, and as for Rose: who can tell?

'What're you wearing tonight, child?' Grandma Sarah, sitting in the rocking chair on the porch looked every inch the pretty old lady Fran had seen rocking on similar porches in a dozen movies.

'My best dress, of course,' said Fran, 'but you'll be the belle of the ball.'

Grandma Sarah laughed. 'I always was, you know. Didn't Mary tell you that?'

Fran took a moment to realise that Grandma Sarah was speaking of her own great-grandmother, now dead.

'Yes, she did, of course. And showed me photographs.'

Grandma Sarah sighed. 'Things would've been quite different now if only . . .'

'If only what?'

'If only I hadn't set my cap for Grandpa. He was Mary's beau, you know. I figure that was why she upped and ran away to England. Poor Mary. I guess it wasn't a kind thing to do, but if you'd seen him in those days . . . Lordy, Lordy, what a man!' Grandma Sarah rocked backwards and forwards and closed her eyes. 'Harry has the look of him. I can see him all over again.'

Fran tried to make the connection. Harry? Golden Harry and the wrinkled, shrivelled old man in the loud print shirts the same? Would Harry look like that? Ever? She couldn't believe it.

'You not saying a thing, eh?' Grandma Sarah chuckled. 'You've got it bad, I guess. Am I right?'

'I don't know what you mean, Grandma Sarah.'

'I mean Harry. You fancy you're in love with him. I don't blame you, honey, only watch yourself.'

'You and Grandpa seem OK.' Fran decided not to deny it. 'Sixty years together and everything.'

'Don't let that fool you, Fran. It's no picnic, being married to a man who's like some kind of candle.'

'I don't understand . . . why a candle?'

'Why, they burn so bright that all the moths around just can't help it, they keep coming near and getting burned.'

'Moths?' Fran was finding herself more and more confused.

'Other women.' Grandma Sarah paused. 'They never stop trying to get close. And they succeed, too, sometimes. They get their wings singed in the end, but some of them . . . well, they get . . . they stick around for a while . . . it's no picnic. Don't let the sixty years baloney blind you to that. It's not been one long bed of roses, no sir.'

Fran understood at last. 'But it's you he loves,' she said. 'Isn't
it? Here you are together after all those years. Aren't you
happy?'

'Sure I'm happy now, child. There's no one going to steal him
away now!' She smiled. 'But you watch yourself with Harry.
He's the same. A candle, if ever I saw one.'

Grandma Sarah closed her eyes and before long Fran could
tell from her even breathing, she was asleep. The camera was on
the table beside her. Fran picked it up and took a shot of her
great-grandmother's sister as she lay in the rocking chair.

3:45 p.m. CLOSE-UP. GRANDMA SARAH
The white back of the rocking chair is like a halo around
Grandma Sarah's white hair. The wrinkles are there, and the
grey hair, but so is the delicate nose, and the fine mouth and
the soft curves of cheek and brow. And Grandma Sarah is
slim. Not as supple as she used to be when she was young –
of course not. But much the same shape. Only her feet really
betray her. She is wearing slippers over toes that are gnarled
and bent like tiny tree roots. Fran saw them once, although
they are generally hidden away. Grandma Sarah prefers to
remember them as they were: tucked out of sight in satin
pumps with diamanté buckles and thin heels. She wears a
wedding ring and no other jewellery, although she has plenty,
upstairs in her bedroom. She no longer has on the lace blouse
she wore for the Family Group. The high neck must have
been stifling in this weather. She has changed into cream
slacks and a loose cotton top the colour of the wisteria that
droops over the roof of the porch and casts a shadow over her
hands, clasped unmoving in her lap.

Gene and Fran were pedalling slowly back to the house. 'I don't
know why I agreed to this ride,' Fran said. 'It's too hot. Why
didn't we stay by the pool?'

'I dunno,' said Gene. 'I like getting out of there sometimes,
going off somewhere . . . it gets to be too . . . demanding. Especially today. We'd have been sucked in if we'd stuck around.
To set the table or put up the bunting or string lights all over the
porch or something.'

'Maybe we should have helped . . .' Fran began.

'We'll say we were being considerate, getting out from under their feet . . . it's OK. Don't worry about it.'

'Can we stop for a bit?' Fran said. 'I need a breather. Is there any Coke left?'

'It'll be hot, though,' said Gene. 'After sitting in the basket for so long.'

'That's OK. I'm used to it,' said Fran. 'Cokes are always warm in England.'

'Is that right?' Gene laughed. 'Sounds a real weird place. The more you tell me about it the weirder it sounds.'

'The beer is warm too,' Fran said.

'You kidding me? Boy, am I glad we got our Independence!'

They sat down by the side of the road in the shade of a tree and drank in silence. Fran lay back on the grass and closed her eyes. When Gene spoke, his voice seemed to come to her from a distance.

'Hey, Fran,' he said. 'When you go back there, to that weird England of yours . . .' He stopped.

'Yes?'

'Well, will you write to me?'

'Would you write back?'

'Sure I would.'

Fran sat up and looked at Gene, who was staring out at the road with his back to her. She said, 'You don't look like a letter writer to me.'

'Don't think I ever wrote a letter in my life before, but I'd write to you.'

Fran smiled. Since Harry had told her of Gene's feelings for her, a lot of the things Gene had said over the days had fallen into a recognisable shape. She had thought he was simply being friendly, but now she understood. What she had difficulty in understanding was her own reaction. She felt – there was only one word for it – powerful. As if she could ask Gene for whatever she wanted and he would give it to her, as though she were a magnet, drawing him. It was quite a pleasant sensation, and she wondered if this was how Harry felt all the time, towards everyone, and how she would behave in his place. Thinking about all this made her feel dizzy: a word from her could hurt Gene. If he knew how she felt about his brother, what would he say? Do? I don't want to hurt him, he's too nice, she thought. He *is* nice. He's not even bad-looking, though he's not Harry, but he's a boy. He's six months younger than me, and small and thin, so he looks even younger. And Harry . . . Harry's a man.

'Yes,' she said. 'Of course I'll write to you. I'm a very good letter writer, as it happens. You'll keep me up to date with all the family news, OK?' (Harry's news – lots of that . . .)

'You want bulletins about Grandma Sarah's rose garden and Susan's latest diet and you want to know if Jean elopes with the bank manager and runs away to Venezuela, that kind of thing?'

'Just news. You know.'

'Right. I guess I could cope with that.'

'Anyway, I'm not leaving till Thursday. That's four days still.'

'Don't remind me.'

'Why not?' (Oh, this awful power, making her do it. Making her want to crack open Gene's secret and find his feeling for her, wanting him to tell her . . . Why? What was she going to do if he did say something? Would she tell him about Harry? What? How?)

Gene considered the question. 'Because I'll miss you. It's been so great having you here . . . showing you things . . . just doing things together.'

Fran felt a sudden wave of affection and tenderness rush over her. She wanted to ruffle his hair and hug him to her as if he were her child. She said, 'I've had fun too, Gene. Really. And of course I'll miss you.' She took his hand and gave it a squeeze.

'Fran . . .' His voice shook. 'Do you have a boyfriend or something . . . in England?'

I should say yes, Fran thought. I should lie. I really should. It would get me out of the situation so neatly. Lie, go on, lie.

'No,' said Fran. 'There's no one in England.'

'Then can I go ahead and kiss you?'

Fran laughed. 'I don't know. Are you supposed to ask? Is that how it's done?'

'I guess the usual way is, you fall into my arms and it just kind of happens, like in the movies, without a word being said. But I don't seem to get into those kind of situations. So I've got to ask you, Fran. Do you mind?'

'What? The asking or the kissing?' (Stop, she cried out to herself, stop tormenting him! Look how anxious he looks . . . oh, Gene, I don't mean to hurt you.)

She put her arm around his shoulder and he turned to her. She closed her eyes. Gene was trembling as he kissed her. She could feel the bones of his shoulders through the hot cotton of his T-shirt, trembling.

Afterwards he said, 'I can't think of a word to say, which is unusual for me.'

'We'd better go back now,' Fran said. 'I bet they will want us to lay the table or something.'

They got on to the bicycles and rode along in silence. Then Gene said, 'Know what I want to do?'

'What?'

'I want to go back and lock myself in my room and play those few seconds back there over and over again, like some kind of video in my head.'

'Why, that's –' Fran bit her lip. That's how I felt, she'd been going to say. This morning with Harry. Tonight, she'd sit between Harry and Gene and not know where to put herself. If only I were at home, she thought suddenly, far away from all of them. She'd never realised living in Paradise would have such problems. On the other hand, she reasoned, all the others would be there. I won't be alone with either of them. I'll worry what to do tomorrow. Tonight I'm going to enjoy the party.

'I'll put the bikes away,' Gene said as they approached the garage.

'Can I take a photo of you first?' said Fran. 'Just standing by the bike?'

'OK.' Gene struck a pose. 'Like this?'

'No,' said Fran. 'Just normal, please.'

'You got it,' he said and grinned, just as Fran pressed the button.

5:00 p.m. CLOSE-UP. GENE
His faded blue T-shirt hangs outside his jeans. It is none too
clean. Neither are the jeans. There are holes at the knees. On
his feet he wears trainers that used once to be white. He has

pushed back the silky fringe of light brown hair that usually falls over his face and left a dirty mark on his forehead in the process. But his teeth are white and straight, and his grey eyes are shining (with love? with laughter? Both). The bike is gleaming. Gene may not take great pains with his own appearance, but it's clear he lavishes all the time and attention in the world on anything he cares about.

Fran looked at herself in the mirror and hardly recognised the image that shone back at her.

'Is that me?' she asked Eleanor. 'I can't believe it. Thank you so much. You wouldn't think just putting up a few strands of hair and twisting it this way and that could make such a difference. I feel grown-up.' She sighed with satisfaction and turned to Eleanor, who bent down and hugged her.

'You look real pretty, Fran. That's a lovely dress too.'

'I don't look as pretty as you. I never will.'

'Why, that's the nicest thing anyone's said to me for the longest time. I love my boys to bits, but you know, I wish I had a girl sometimes. I really miss not having a daughter.'

'And I wish —' Fran stopped. She had been about to say: 'I wish I had a mother like you, who'd put my hair up in loops and spirals and lend me her pearl necklace for parties,' but a sense of guilty loyalty to her own mother prevented her. What would she be doing tonight? Sitting on the old sofa in her rust-coloured cardigan and reading the Sunday papers? Watching television?

'Mom!' came a shout from just outside the door. Harry. 'You in there? Can I come in?' Eleanor looked at Fran, who nodded. Without waiting for permission Harry burst in, pushing his wheelchair across the carpet at high speed.

'Mom, guess who phoned? Ronnie . . . can you believe it? And she's here . . . she just got back. Anyway, I asked Patti, and she said OK, why not, and so I asked her to come over tonight for the party. Isn't that great? Isn't that fantastic?' Without waiting for an answer, he turned the wheelchair round and glided out of the room.

Fran turned back to face the mirror. The image that had pleased her so much only moments before now disgusted her. Harry didn't look at her, didn't even see her. He was taken up with this Ronnie. Who was she? Why had no one mentioned her? And how dare she just turn up like this and muscle in on a family occasion?

'That's wonderful for Harry,' Eleanor said. 'He and Ronnie are so fond of each other.'

'Is she his girlfriend?' Fran forced her voice into a kind of steadiness. Eleanor laughed.

'Harry has girlfriends like other guys have shirts. One for each day of the week. But Ronnie's special to him, I guess. Wait till you see her. You'll see why.'

Fran struggled not to cry. If she cried, her mascara would run. If she cried, everyone would know. She felt a moment of pure loathing for pretty, unconcerned Eleanor, who was clever about hair and make-up and so stupid she couldn't see how Fran felt about her son.

'I'd better go down now and help with the table,' she said.

'Just wait one second,' said Eleanor. 'I'm going to take a photo of you right now, just as you are. You look so terrific.' She picked up the camera from Fran's bedside table. 'Sit where you are, right there on the stool and look up at me. That's it.'

Eleanor focused on Fran's face and pressed the button.

'Hey, will you look at that!' she cried. 'I'm in the shot as well. In the mirror. Gee, Fran honey, I'm sorry. Why didn't I think of that?'

'It doesn't matter, honestly,' Fran said. 'Actually, I think it looks interesting like that.'

'You're being polite,' Eleanor smiled. 'I guess that's because you're British.'

7:00 p.m. CLOSE-UP. FRAN, WITH ELEANOR
The lamp on the dressing-table has edged Fran's hair with gold. Her eyes are shadowed and she is unsmiling. The silky material of her dress falls over her shoulders in folds of scarlet and the pearls round her neck shine from the warmth of her skin. Behind her in the mirror you can see Eleanor, taking the photograph. Her red hair falls over the camera. Her dress is made of chiffon: turquoise, blue, green, mauve blending in an ocean of colour. Also reflected are the wall-lights above Eleanor's head: small, cream lampshades fringed with tassels.

A field of soft, pink carpet stretches away to the door.

'I don't think,' said Susan, 'I'm ever going to eat another morsel as long as I live.'

Gene bent towards Fran and whispered: 'Five'll get you ten she'll have buckwheat pancakes for breakfast. Wait and see.'

Fran giggled. She had been giggling a lot: from the seafood salad, through the roast prime ribs, right up to the strawberry shortcake. It must be the wine, she thought vaguely. She looked at Gene, beside her. She looked at Harry and Ronnie, sitting right across the table from her. Ronnie. When she'd first met her before dinner, about a hundred years ago, Fran felt the shock of recognition, Ronnie was the female equivalent of Harry. Miss Golden. She and Harry fitted like two halves of a torn dollar bill. Look at the way she dressed! A black and white pinstriped suit, like a Chicago gangster (in June, for goodness sake!), worn with a black and white checked shirt. Stripes and checks together – the daring of it took Fran's breath away. Ronnie had straight, blonde hair, cut like a boy's, a wide mouth and a skin like all the words in all the make-up advertisements in the world. Fran drank wine, all the wine she was offered, to blur the truth which she knew and couldn't bear. This Ronnie, whoever she was, was Something Else. A different league. Almost a different species from herself. She turned to Gene for consolation.

'Isn't Ronnie lovely?' she whispered.

Gene considered. He took a bite of seafood salad and swallowed it. 'She's OK,' he said. 'If you like the Robert Redford type.'

That's when Fran started giggling. Everyone ate too much. There was too much talk. Reminiscences. Fran listened and giggled and looked around. The strawberry shortcake was in ruins: crumbs and blobby bits of cream lay about on the plate, and the rosebuds had long ago fallen off on to the white lace of Grandma Sarah's best tablecloth.

'I think I'm drunk,' Fran said to Gene. 'I'm seeing things.'

'What things?'

'I can't describe it . . . it's strange.' For a moment, or maybe for longer, Fran had felt as if she were a long way away, up on the ceiling, perhaps, and looking down on to the table. The people had vanished and only their clothes were left: clothes sitting up in chairs. There was Rose's black lace, leaning over to talk to Joe's tuxedo. Susan's yellow dress billowed over the table. Jean's wine-coloured silk and Patti's beige, Eleanor's sea-coloured chiffon and Grandma Sarah's lavender velvet, draped themselves this way and that. And the arm of Harry's jacket was around the shoulders of a Chicago gangster suit in black and white stripes, right across the table from a red silky dress that was sitting up very straight in its chair.

'Fran honey, where's that magic box of yours?' Grandpa looked down the table at her.

'I'll get it, Grandpa,' said Fran. 'It's in my bedroom.'

'It's OK,' said Gene. 'I'll get it. You'll fall over if you try and get up.'

'I won't,' said Fran weakly, but Gene had gone.

When he returned there was a debate about who should take the picture. Back and forth the talk went, over the crumbs and the patterns in the tablecloth. In the end Fran spoke:

'Listen, Grandpa,' she said, 'it's my camera and I'm taking this picture. So there.' The wine had given her courage.

She stood, rather unsteadily, at the end of the table and looked at them all. They were smiling.

'Watch the birdie,' she said.

10:00 p.m. THE DINING ROOM.
ANNIVERSARY DINNER

Everyone is smiling. What does it mean? Grandpa's smile says: I made it. I'm eighty-four and still here and so's Sarah, and these are my children and my grandchild and great-grandchildren and even a branch of the family tree from England, flown over specially for the occasion, like a florist's delivery. Grandma Sarah's smile is wistful. I'm a good-looking old lady, it says, sure, but for how much longer? She seems to be glancing at Ronnie as if at her own past. Susan's smile is brave − her corset is pinching like hell. Rose's is a little forced. She is smiling at Bill, who smiles obediently back at her. Jean is enigmatic as usual, a Mona Lisa smile. Eleanor grins proudly, and so she should, looking at her sons. Harry smiles at Ronnie. Possessively. She looks happy, happy with

*herself and with Harry, and with good reason. Gene is
smiling straight at the camera. Or, and this is more likely, at
the person holding the camera. He is smiling at Fran and his
eyes look as if they're pleased with what they're seeing.*

'It's OK, Fran, honey. Honest, it's OK. Really.' Gene was
pleading. 'You don't have to cry. You don't have to feel bad
about it. It's nothing to be ashamed of. You just had too much
to drink, is all. I've cleaned up after people before . . . at camp
and even right here. Why, I clean up after Harry all the time.'

Fran burst into fresh paroxysms of tears. 'Don't tell Harry,'
she begged, 'please don't tell Harry I threw up. I couldn't bear it.'

Gene looked at her, puzzled. 'I won't if you don't want me to.
But it beats me why not. You OK now? Come on into the
kitchen and I'll get you a cup of coffee.'

'My head hurts,' said Fran.

'Sure it does. Hurt even worse in the morning. You wait.'

'That's terrific. You certainly know how to cheer a person up.'

'I'm just a little ray of sunshine. Didn't you know? C'mon.'

In the kitchen, they drank coffee sitting at the table.

'I still get a kick staying up late, d'you know that?' Gene said.
'I guess it means I'm not an adult yet.'

'I feel as if I could sleep for a week.' She paused. 'Gene, I want
to tell you something.'

'Shoot.'

'Back there, it wasn't just the food and the drink, you
know . . . it was something I saw. I shouldn't tell you really,
only I must speak about it. I'm sorry, Gene. You see, I went out
to sit by the pool, just to get a bit of air and I suppose I was
feeling a bit drunk and then . . .'

'Go on.'

'Well,' Fran gulped at her coffee. 'Harry and Ronnie were out
there. They were . . . well . . . kissing. I mean, they didn't even
see me or hear me they were so . . . taken up with one another. I
just fled. I couldn't look.'

'That made you throw up? Seriously? You mean because of
Harry? You figured I didn't know what you felt about him?
You're crazy, Fran. It sticks out a mile. I knew before you did, I
guess.'

'Didn't it bother you? After . . . well, I mean, I thought you liked me and everything.'

'No percentage being jealous of Harry any more than being jealous of a flower or the Grand Canyon or something like that. Anyway, I'm an optimist. I reckoned after you kissed me, I'd quit being a frog and turn into a prince for you, right there on the spot.'

Fran laughed. 'This morning you were an ugly duckling.'

'And you said I'd turn into a swan eventually.' Gene stood up and pirouetted round the floor. 'How'm I doing?'

'I like you so much, Gene,' Fran said. 'You're so nice and funny and kind . . .'

'. . . and handsome and clever. Go on. Don't stop there.'

Fran looked down at her empty coffee cup. She said, 'I want to explain about Harry. I thought this morning that I loved him, but I can see it now . . . it wasn't love. It was more like being dazzled . . . it wasn't altogether real . . . I can't explain it. It was like a picture of love, a dream of it, a sort of fantasy on my part. I mean, this whole place doesn't seem like the real world to me. It's difficult for an American to understand, I know, but for me and for a lot of people who've never been here, the whole place is like a movie we carry round in our heads. Or a hundred different movies: Western plains, city streets, beaches full of surfers, Southern plantations – everything. And Harry's part of that. All tied up with that. Even this house and all of you, even though you're family, seem . . . I don't know . . . remote from my ordinary life. When I'm here, I find it difficult to think about school, and my own little bedroom and the small square of grass that's my garden.'

'What about me? Am I a dream, too?' Gene asked quietly.

'No, you're real. You're the only one of the whole lot of them I can picture coming down to the chip shop with me . . . riding on the bus to school with me.'

'I'll do that!' Gene's face lit up. 'Next summer. You wait. I'll be over there, wait and see, and we'll ride all the buses you like and you can feed me warm Cokes. I won't care. I mean it. I'm coming. You expect me. OK?'

Fran smiled in spite of herself. 'How can you be so sure?'

'Well, now, you see. It's a family tradition. Seventeen years old, you get a ticket to Europe. Grandpa practically insists. Only, I'm going to skip all that art galleries and cathedrals jazz and just concentrate on England. I can't wait.'

'It'll be wonderful if it happens . . .' Fran yawned.

Gene said: 'It will. I promise . . .' and then the door opened and Jean came in and grinned at them.

'You kids still up? Do you know what time it is? Look at you . . . you look a real mess, both of you. Bed. Right now.'

'Aw, Jean, c'mon. I don't feel like sleeping . . . hey, do you realise we have the same name? I feel like I'm talking to myself.' Gene laughed and whispered to Fran: 'Tomorrow night I'll take you to a drive-in movie.' He put his arm around her shoulders and pulled her towards him, whispered in her ear: 'You know . . . we'll kiss so much, we won't see much of what's going on. It's a real old American cliché. You'll just love it!'

'Are you kids through fooling around?' Jean said. 'I'm supposed to be locking up around here.'

Fran giggled and clung to Gene. 'Will you take a photo of us, please?' she said.

Jean laughed. 'You must be out of your mind, Fran. Have you seen what you look like? Whoever takes photos at two in the morning anyway?'

'Please, Jean, it's very important.'

'If it's going to get you guys out of the kitchen, I'll do anything. Go on, then. Smile or something.'

Gene and Fran smiled at one another.

2:00 a.m. CLOSE-UP. FRAN AND GENE
Fran's hair has come down. All the party spirals and curls are hanging round her shoulders. Gene has the sleeves of his evening shirt turned up above the elbows. Also, his tie has disappeared. The shirt is open at the neck. One hand is in Fran's hair, lifting it up a little. Fran looks pale, but she is smiling and so is Gene. No one would know that they'd asked for this picture to be taken. It's as though the photographer didn't exist, as though the camera has caught them off guard just at that moment – seeing one another properly for the very first time. Knowing.

Personal Essay
by Adèle Geras

A short story is a piece of prose that isn't long enough to be a novel – and even this statement is not quite true. Some short stories are as long as pieces of fiction I have written and called novels. Ten lines of an Aesop fable is as much a short story as an elaborate word-tapestry from the needle/pen of Henry James.

Every short story is unique: one of a kind. Every short story presents its writer with new problems and the short stories you've written in the past are generally of little help. There are, of course, broad categories of story: after you've written a few, you can probably say into which categories your own stories fall and which kind you most enjoy writing. Let me list a few:

1   The story as an extended anecdote/joke with a strong punch-line or a dramatic twist in the tail.
2   The story as a glimpse through a window, a small slice of a largely unknown life.
3   The 'what if?' story. A great deal of horror and science fiction writing falls into this category. Take an idea, the author thinks, and stretch it as far as it'll go without snapping.
4   The prose poem. This is usually an extended description, perhaps of a landscape, to convey a feeling or evoke a mood.
5   The character study. This is a glimpse through a microscope at one person in often quite absorbing detail.
6   The 'Ancient Mariner' type. These stories are always in the first person, with a strong author's voice speaking directly to you and not letting you move till the story is over. Damon Runyan was an American writer of the 1930s who wrote of small time crooks, not-very-efficient gamblers and their assorted lady friends in such an individual way that you can almost 'hear' the words on the page. How's this for a first sentence? It comes from a story called 'Tobias the Terrible':
> 'One night I am sitting in Mindy's restaurant on Broadway partaking heartily of some Hungarian goulash which comes very nice in Mindy's, what with the chef being personally somewhat Hungarian himself, when in pops a guy who is a stranger to me and sits at my table.'
7   The small drama. This is more like a short play than anything else. Something happens to someone, someone does something, feels something, says something to another person, and some kind of change or resolution is achieved.

Seven broad categories. There are probably more. I've written 'what-if' ghost stories, and a couple of Ancient Mariners, but I like small dramas best. There are no wild fantasies, no immensely detailed characters, no 'gasp-I-never-would-have-guessed-it' amazement at the end, just a scene, or a series of scenes with A BEGINNING, A MIDDLE, AND AN END though not (as someone once said) necessarily in that order.

Time in the story does not have to be linear and writers have all kinds of fun writing stories that start in a person's old age and work back to their youth, or stories that jump about among the years like spring lambs. We are now so used to cinematic and television techniques (the flashback, the voice-over, the dissolve) that as readers, we can take such tricks in our stride.

I like writing short stories for two reasons. Reason One is a good, right-thinking Reason: always immaculately dressed and polite to everyone. Top of the class and a prefect in all probability. Here she is: short stories help you to perfect techniques, to work on your ideas, to try things out, to extend your horizons, to learn about the craft of writing.

Reason Two wears darned denims, holey trainers, and has been known to chew gum. She reads rubbishy magazines and never hands her homework in on time. Here she is: short stories are *Short*. You can finish one in a couple of hours. Hooray! Up go the feet, on goes the TV, this is the life!

Short stories are ideal for people who like to get a thing finished, the kind of person who likes knitting sleeveless pullovers on huge needles. Novels take over your life for months, and you can't hold a whole novel in your head. A short story is something your mind can grasp – a whole small thing.

When my collection of love stories, *The Green behind the Glass* was to be published in the United States, the publishers asked for a story with an American 'angle'. This is how 'Snapshots of Paradise' came to be written. I'd visited New York when I was eleven years old, for one month, and therefore didn't count myself an expert on the subject. I thought it best to present the story from a visitor's point of view for that reason. I'm fascinated by photographs in general and those magic instant pictures in particular, and visitors to a country take a lot of those. I liked the idea of different generations of a family gathered together. I like contrasts (youth/old age, light/dark, appearance/reality, past tense for narrative/present tense for photographs). I like meals and the preparation of meals. I like clothes and what they hide and reveal about people. As I write, I can visualise the scene I'm writing about in my mind. In some stories, the writer has one bright hoop to show you, one coloured scarf to draw out of the conjuror's hat. In 'Snapshots of Paradise' I was conscious of juggling, of having set a lot of plates spinning in the air, and of trying not to let any of them crash to the ground. I hope it's worked. Finally, I have to admit to a sneaking affection for the 'plain-girl/boy-turns-out-to-be-Ms/Mr Right-in-the-end' kind of story. Happy endings are getting to be as rare in fiction as in real life, so I enjoyed writing a joyful story for a change.

The last word for anyone who wants to write. Look at everything. Listen to people as they speak, watch the way they move. Read everything you can lay hands on. Be honest. Tell it like it is for you, even if (especially if) it's the most way-out fantasy. Try out voices. Improvise on paper. Try and write *something* every day, as if writing were a muscle that needed exercise. The greatest story in the world is nothing locked up inside your head. *Write it down now.* Then put your feet up!

ENDS

KRISTIN HUNTER

Debut

'Hold *still*, Judy,' Mrs Simmons said around the spray of pins that protruded dangerously from her mouth. She gave the thirtieth tug to the tight sash at the waist of the dress. 'Now walk over there and turn around slowly.'

The dress, Judy's first long one, was white organdie over taffeta, with spaghetti straps that bared her round brown shoulders and a floating skirt and a wide sash that cascaded in a butterfly effect behind. It was a dream, but Judy was sick and tired of the endless fittings she had endured so that she might wear it at the Debutante's Ball. Her thoughts leaped ahead to the Ball itself . . .

'*Slowly*, I said!' Mrs Simmons' dark, angular face was always grim, but now it was screwed into an expression resembling a prune. Judy, starting nervously, began to revolve by moving her feet an inch at a time.

Her mother watched her critically. 'No, it's still not right. I'll just have to rip out that waistline seam again.'

'Oh, Mother!' Judy's impatience slipped out at last. 'Nobody's going to notice all those little details.'

'They will too. They'll be watching you every minute, hoping to see something wrong. You've got to be the *best*. Can't you get that through your head?' Mrs Simmons gave a sigh of

60

despair. 'You better start noticin' "all those little details" your-self. I can't do it for you all your life. Now turn around and stand up straight.'

'Oh, Mother,' Judy said, close to tears from being made to turn and pose while her feet itched to be dancing, 'I can't stand it any more!'

'You can't stand it, huh? How do you think *I* feel?' Mrs Simmons said in her harshest tone.

Judy was immediately ashamed, remembering the weeks her mother had spent at the sewing machine, pricking her already tattered fingers with needles and pins, and the great weight of sacrifice that had been borne on Mrs Simmons' shoulders for the past two years so that Judy might bare hers at the Ball.

'All right, take it off,' her mother said. 'I'm going to take it up the street to Mrs Luby and let her help me. It's got to be right or I won't let you leave the house.'

'Can't we just leave it the way it is, Mother?' Judy pleaded without hope of success. 'I think it's perfect.'

'You would,' Mrs Simmons said tartly as she folded the dress and prepared to bear it out of the room. 'Sometimes I think I'll never get it through your head. You got to look just right and act just right. That Rose Griffin and those other girls can afford to be careless, maybe, but you can't. You're gonna be the darkest, poorest one there.'

Judy shivered in her new lace strapless bra and her old, childish knit snuggies. 'You make it sound like a battle I'm going to instead of just a dance.'

'It is a battle,' her mother said firmly. 'It starts tonight and it goes on for the rest of your life. The battle to hold your head up and get someplace and be somebody. We've done all we can for you, your father and I. Now you've got to start fighting some on your own.' She gave Judy a slight smile; her voice softened a little. 'You'll do all right, don't worry. Try and get some rest this afternoon. Just don't mess up your hair.'

'All right, Mother,' Judy said listlessly.

She did not really think her father had much to do with anything that happened to her. It was her mother who had ingratiated her way into the Gay Charmers two years ago, taking all sorts of humiliation from the better-dressed, better-off, lighter-skinned women, humbly making and mending their dresses, fixing food for their meetings, addressing more mail and selling more tickets than anyone else. The club had put it off as long as they could, but finally they had to admit Mrs Simmons to membership because she worked so hard. And that meant, of course, that Judy would be on the list for this year's Ball.

Her father, a quiet carpenter who had given up any other ambitions years ago, did not think much of society or his wife's fierce determination to launch Judy into it. 'Just keep clean and be decent,' he would say. 'That's all anybody has to do.'

Her mother always answered, 'If that's all *I* did we'd still be on relief,' and he would shut up with shame over the years when he had been laid off repeatedly and her days' work and sewing had kept them going. Now he had steady work but she refused to quit, as if she expected it to end at any moment. The intense energy that burned in Mrs Simmons' large dark eyes had scorched her features into permanent irony. She worked day and night and spent her spare time scheming and planning. Whatever her personal ambitions had been, Judy knew she blamed Mr Simmons for their failure; now all her schemes revolved around their only child.

Judy went to her mother's window and watched her stride down the street with the dress until she was hidden by the high brick wall that went around two sides of their house. Then she returned to her own room. She did not get dressed because she was afraid of pulling a sweater over her hair – her mother would notice the difference even if it looked all right to Judy – and because she was afraid that doing anything, even getting dressed, might precipitate her into the battle. She drew a stool up to her window and looked out. She had no real view, but she liked her room. The wall hid the crowded tenement houses beyond the alley, and from its cracks and bumps and depressions she could construct any imaginary landscape she chose. It was how she had spent most of the free hours of her dreamy adolescence.

'Hey, can I go?'

It was the voice of an invisible boy in the alley. As another boy chuckled, Judy recognised the familiar ritual; if you said yes, they said, 'Can I go with you?' It had been tried on her dozens of times. She always walked past, head in the air, as if she had not heard. Her mother said that was the only thing to do; if they knew she was a lady, they wouldn't dare bother her. But this time a girl's voice, cool and assured, answered.

'If you think you're big enough,' it said.

It was Lucy Mae Watkins; Judy could picture her standing there in a tight dress with bright, brazen eyes.

'I'm big enough to give you a baby,' the boy answered.

Judy would die if a boy ever spoke to her like that, but she knew Lucy Mae could handle it. Lucy Mae could handle all the boys, even if they ganged up on her, because she had been born knowing something other girls had to learn.

'Aw, you ain't big enough to give me a shoe-shine,' she told him.

'Come here and I'll show you how big I am,' the boy said.

'Yeah, Lucy Mae, what's happenin'?' another boy said. 'Come here and tell us.'

Lucy Mae laughed. 'What I'm puttin' down is too strong for little boys like you.'

'Come here a minute, baby,' the first boy said. 'I got a cigarette for you.'

'Aw, I ain't studyin' your cigarettes,' Lucy Mae answered. But her voice was closer, directly below Judy. There were the sounds of a scuffle and Lucy Mae's muffled laughter. When she spoke her voice sounded raw and cross. 'Come on now, boy. Cut it out and give me the damn cigarette.' There was more scuffling, and the sharp crack of a slap, and then Lucy Mae said, 'Cut it out, I said. Just for that I'm gonna take 'em all.' The clack of high heels rang down the sidewalk with a boy's clumsy shoes in pursuit.

Judy realised that there were three of them down there. 'Let her go, Buster,' one said. 'You can't catch her now.'

'Aw, hell, man, she took the whole damn pack,' the one called Buster complained.

'That'll learn you!' Lucy Mae's voice mocked from down the street. 'Don't mess with nothin' you can't handle.'

'Hey, Lucy Mae. Hey, I heard Rudy Grant already gave you a baby,' a second boy called out.

'Yeah. Is that true, Lucy Mae?' the youngest one yelled.

There was no answer. She must be a block away by now.

For a moment the hidden boys were silent; then one of them guffawed directly below Judy, and the other two joined in the secret male laughter that was oddly high-pitched and feminine.

'Aw man, I don't know what you all laughin' about,' Buster finally grumbled. 'That girl took all my cigarettes. You got some, Leroy?'

'Naw,' the second boy said.

'What we gonna do? I ain't got but fifteen cents. Hell, man, I want more than a feel for a pack of cigarettes.' There was an unpleasant whine in Buster's voice. 'Hell, for a pack of cigarettes I want a bitch to come across.'

'She will next time,' Buster said. 'You know she better. If she pass by here again, we gonna jump her, you hear?'

'Sure, man,' Leroy said. 'The three of us can grab her easy.'

'Then we can all three of us have some fun. Oh, *yeah*, man,' the youngest boy said. He sounded as if he might be about fourteen.

Leroy said, 'We oughta get Roland and J. T. too. For a whole pack of cigarettes she oughta treat all five of us.'

'Aw, man, why tell Roland and J. T.?' the youngest voice whined. 'They ain't in it. Them was *our* cigarettes.'

'They was *my* cigarettes, you mean,' Buster said with authority. 'You guys better quit it before I decide to cut you out.'

'Oh, man, don't do that. We with you. You know that.'

'Sure, Buster, we your aces, man.'

'All right, that's better.' There was a minute of silence.

Then, 'What we gonna do with the girl, Buster?' the youngest one wanted to know.

'When she come back we gonna jump the bitch, man. We gonna jump her and grab her. Then we gonna turn her every way but loose.' He went on, spinning a crude fantasy that got wilder each time he retold it, until it became so secretive that their voices dropped to a low indistinct murmur punctuated by guffaws. Now and then Judy could distinguish the word 'girl' or the other word they used for it; these words always produced the loudest guffaws of all. She shook off her fear with the thought that Lucy Mae was too smart to pass there again today.

She had heard them at their dirty talk in the alley before and had always been successful in ignoring it; it had nothing to do with her, the wall protected her from their kind. All the ugliness was on their side of it, and this side was hers to fill with beauty.

She turned on her radio to shut them out completely and began to weave her tapestry to its music. More for practice than anything else, she started by picturing the maps of the places to which she intended to travel, then went on to the faces of her friends. Rose Griffin's sharp, Indian profile appeared on the wall. Her colouring was like an Indian's too and her hair was straight and black and glossy. Judy's hair, naturally none of these things, had been 'done' four days ago so that tonight it would be 'old' enough to have a gloss as natural-looking as Rose's. But Rose, despite her handsome looks, was silly; her voice broke constantly into high-pitched giggles and she became even sillier and more nervous around boys.

Judy was not sure that she knew how to act around boys either. The sisters kept boys and girls apart at the Catholic high school where her parents sent her to keep her away from low-class kids. But she felt that she knew a secret: tonight, in that dress, with her hair in a sophisticated upsweep, she would be transformed into a poised princess. Tonight all the college boys her mother described so eagerly would rush to dance with her, and then from somewhere *the boy* would appear. She did not know his name; she neither knew nor cared whether he went to college, but she imagined that he would be as dark as she was, and that there would be awe and diffidence in his manner as he bent to kiss her hand . . .

A waltz swelled from the radio; the wall, turning blue in deepening twilight, came alive with whirling figures. Judy rose and began to go through the steps she had rehearsed for so many weeks. She swirled with a practised smile on her face, holding an imaginary skirt at her side; turned, dipped, and flicked on her bedside lamp without missing a fraction of the beat. Faster and faster she danced with her imaginary partner, to an inner music that was better than the sounds on the radio. She was 'coming out,' and tonight the world would discover what it had been waiting for all these years.

'Aw git it, baby.' She ignored it as she would ignore the

crowds that lined the streets to watch her pass on her way to the Ball.

'Aw, do your number.' She waltzed on, safe and secure on her side of the wall.

'Can I come up there and do it with you?'

At this she stopped, paralysed. Somehow they had come over the wall or around it and into her road.

'Man, I sure like the view from here,' the youngest boy said. 'How come we never tried this view before?'

She came to life, ran quickly to the lamp and turned it off, but not before Buster said, 'Yeah, and the back view is fine, too.'

'Aw, she turned off the light,' a voice complained.

'Put it on again, baby, we don't mean no harm.'

'Let us see you dance some more. I bet you can really do it.'

'Yeah, I bet she can shimmy on down.'

'You know it man.'

'Come on down here, baby,' Buster's voice urged softly, dangerously. 'I got a cigarette for you.'

'Yeah, and he got something else for you, too.'

Judy, flattened against her closet door, gradually lost her urge to scream. She realised that she was shivering in her underwear. Taking a deep breath, she opened the closet door and found her robe. She thought of going to the window and yelling down, 'You don't have anything I want. Do you understand?' But she had more important things to do.

Wrapping her hair in a protective plastic, she ran a full steaming tub and dumped in half a bottle of her mother's favourite cologne. At first she scrubbed herself furiously, irritating her skin. But finally she stopped, knowing she would never be able to get cleaner than this again. She could not wash away the thing they considered dirty, the thing that made them pronounce 'girl' in the same way as the other four-letter words they wrote on the wall in the alley; it was part of her, just as it was part of her mother and Rose Griffin and Lucy Mae. She relaxed then because it was true that the boys in the alley did not have a thing she wanted. She had what they wanted, and the knowledge replaced her shame with a strange, calm feeling of power.

After her bath she splashed on more cologne and spent forty

minutes on her make-up, erasing and retracing her eyebrows six times until she was satisfied. She went to her mother's room then and found the dress, finished and freshly pressed, on its hanger.

When Mrs Simmons came upstairs to help her daughter she found her sitting on the bench before the vanity mirror as if it were a throne. She looked young and arrogant and beautiful and perfect and cold.

'Why, you're dressed already,' Mrs Simmons said in surprise. While she stared, Judy rose with perfect, icy grace and glided to the centre of the room. She stood there motionless as a mannequin.

'I want you to fix the hem, Mother,' she directed. 'It's still uneven at the back.'

Her mother went down obediently on her knees muttering, 'It looks all right to me.' She put in a couple of pins. 'That better?'

'Yes,' Judy said with a brief glance at the mirror. 'You'll have to sew it on me, Mother. I can't take it off now. I'd ruin my hair.'

Mrs Simmons went to fetch her sewing things, returned and surveyed her daughter. 'You sure did a good job on yourself, I must say,' she admitted grudgingly. 'Can't find a thing to complain about. You'll look as good as anybody there.'

'Of course, Mother,' Judy said as Mrs Simmons knelt and sewed. 'I don't know what you were so worried about.' Her secret feeling of confidence had returned, stronger than ever, but the evening ahead was no longer a girlish fantasy she had pictured on the wall; it had hard, clear outlines leading up to a definite goal. She would be the belle of the Ball because she knew more than Rose Griffin and her silly friends; more than her mother, more, even than Lucy Mae, because she knew better than to settle for a mere pack of cigarettes.

'There,' her mother said, breaking the thread. She got up. 'I never expected to get you ready this early. Ernest Lee won't be here for another hour.'

'That silly Ernest Lee,' Judy said, with a new contempt in her young voice. Until tonight she had been pleased by the thought of going to the dance with Ernest Lee; he was nice, she felt comfortable with him, and he might even be the awe-struck boy of her dream. He was a dark, serious neighbourhood boy who could not afford to go to college; Mrs Simmons had reluctantly selected him to take Judy to the dance because all the Gay Charmers' sons were spoken for. Now, with an undertone of excitement, Judy said, 'I'm going to ditch him after the dance, Mother. You'll see. I'm going to come home with one of the college boys.'

'It's very nice, Ernest Lee,' she told him an hour later when he handed her the white orchid, 'but it's rather small. I'm going to wear it on my wrist, if you don't mind.' And then, dazzling him with a smile of sweetest cruelty, she stepped back and waited while he fumbled with the door.

'You know, Edward, I'm not worried about her any more,' Mrs Simmons said to her husband after the children were gone. Her voice became harsh and grating. 'Put down that paper and listen to me! Aren't you interested in your child? – That's better,' she said as he complied meekly. 'I was saying, I do believe she's learned what I've been trying to teach her, after all.'

KYM MARTINDALE

The Kestrels

Claire paused a moment on the moortrack and looked down into the valley. The small mill town crawled straight-backed up the hills, rigid rows of terraces, jagged millroofs and wet slates. There were many tall chimneys too, but their smokeless tops told the tale of unemployment. Claire gazed searchingly at the town. If she used her binoculars, she could perhaps have picked out the school where she should have been and where her friends were now. All except for Jakey, of course.

She turned away and continued up the moortrack. The wind was strong but she enjoyed the challenge. She was glad to pit herself against its aggression. Ever since Jakey had gone, she'd hated everything and everyone. Her schoolfriends, her parents, they seemed like so much trivia beside Jakey and it made her want to hit and smash the world to think of what they'd done. That was why today she'd skived off school and come up here, where she and Jakey always came to watch the kestrels.

She topped the hill and the track started down. In the distance she could already see the old barn where the kestrels nested and for a moment she stopped as a bird flew out from under the eaves. Claire grinned. You could rely on the kestrels.

She watched the bird fly out of sight then clambered over the wall, off the track and towards the field where the barn stood.

She was well settled in a corner by the lee of the old stone wall, when the bird returned.

It made Claire want to cry. The peerless ease and beauty of the kestrel always caught her emotions. But more than that, she wanted Jakey here to share it. Jakey understood. And Jakey loved.

The kestrel swung out again and perched a moment on the top of a telegraph post. Claire focused. She felt she could touch him. His bright eye glittered at her, his colours, smooth and intricate, seemed inches from her fingers. Oh you are so beautiful, she crooned softly. But he was off again, beating into the air, into the distance. She watched him go, then breathed out. Oh Jakey, you should be here.

* * *

A hundred miles away, a girl stood on a slipway to the M6, traffic ignoring her outstretched thumb, wind whipping through her jacket. An hour she'd been here. It was getting cold and she was scared. She'd never hitched and dark half-remembered tales had made her relieved at first when the cars went on past. But now panic was making her throat dry. Please somebody, stop.

Just then, a huge lorry lumbered past, the driver caught her eye and, tail lights winking, the truck finally stopped twenty yards on. Oh thank god, muttered the girl, and ran to the cab, her rucksack banging on her back and her other fear rising in her stomach.

The driver leaned across, opened the door and shouted, 'I can take you as far as Preston, son.' The girl was stumped. Son? Then she saw her boots and jeans through his eyes and grinned. 'Son' was a bonus. Fear quenched, she climbed into the cab.

'Preston is where I'm going, mate,' she said as gruffly as she dared.

'Right we are then,' and the driver eased off the brakes.

The truck lurched forward and the girl suddenly turned to the window. 'Owt wrong?' said the driver.

'No,' she laughed and sat back, 'just saw a kestrel, that's all.'

* * *

Claire took out some sandwiches and a flask. Her hunger was sharp, always was up here and she ate quickly as if someone might snatch the food away. Then she sat back, a steaming cup of tea warming her hands. The kestrel had been away for some time now. She searched the sky again but there was nothing. Jakey would have been impatient, wanting to move. You were always keen to get on to the next thing Jakey, for all your love of the kestrels, you never liked the waiting.

Claire sipped her tea and closed her eyes. I always had to coax you just that little bit, Jakey, but then, it was your impatience that got us started. And Claire lost her hold on her thoughts as memories of Jakey pushed them out. Jakey, new kid at school, Jakey sitting next to her in English, then everything else. Jakey, sharp and thin, weird and beautiful, round for tea, out together on the tops watching the kestrels, all new to Jakey, the city kid; the kestrels, Claire's proud gift to Jakey, with the feelings and fear of the love and the need; then Jakey and Claire in the grass, in the late summer sun by the old wall, Jakey falling against Claire and not moving back, both silent and scared, and Jakey's final burst of impatience, 'Claire, I love you.' Oh, the wonderful desperation in that voice, the look in those eyes and their disbelief when Claire said, 'I love you, too, Jakey.'

She opened her eyes and finished the tea in one gulp. As she packed away her flask she saw the kestrel was back, but she didn't pick up her binoculars. He settled on his post again and began to tear at something in his claws, the choicest of which he'd already given to his mate in the barn. Claire watched him. Tear and chew, and never once letting his glance stray from his surroundings. She spoke to him, soft and low. He was the only living thing she'd tell about Jakey, he became Jakey.

All that love, she said, and I would have let it go but for you. Even so, and she smiled, it took us long enough to get that first kiss out of the way. We just hugged and hugged, terrified of it all, but when we did kiss, Jakey, I just knew it was right.

She wrinkled her nose. It sounded mushy. The kestrel tore and chewed, balancing against the wind, ever on the watch. I wish I could forget you, she told him, but I love you. And for the first time since Jakey had gone, Claire broke down.

We couldn't go on up here, she sobbed to the bird, it got so cold. She stopped as the touch of Jakey came back to her, wow, if folks only knew, and above all, the wonder of being loved.

Now all the folks knew, parents, schoolfriends. A bad phase, they said, yes, separation, it's a good idea. So they sent you away, Jakey, Claire told the kestrel; but the bird had finished his meal and flown away.

* * *

'Platform one, sonny, you got two minutes.'

'Cheers,' the girl shouted above the noise and began to run. She'd had a good hitch, right outside the station the driver had let her off. She hurried through the clanking, hissing, echoing platforms. Her train was ready to go, the guard saw her and jerked open a door with a grin. Breathlessly she stumbled in and, as the door slammed, she heard the guard say, 'Just in time, son.'

The girl straightened up and leaned out of the window.

'I'm not a boy,' she shouted, 'I'm a woman.' There was hardly time to enjoy his expression as the train slid forward and she fell back, laughing until she could have cried, and never believing the train could carry her fast enough.

* * *

The light was beginning to fail and Claire's body was stiff. She'd have to go soon, but it had been a good day for the kestrels. They'd both been out and Claire began to feel excited about the time when the young would hatch.

But now the dark was growing and lights were glowing faintly in the valley. She rose awkwardly and stretched, and threw her bag over her shoulder. She looked at the barn. See you soon, she murmured to the quiet building, then she turned and clambered over the wall.

* * *

Far down the moortrack, the girl ran jerkily, thin legs leaping over the puddles, her breath coming short. The train had been late. Hell, she muttered savagely, I have to be in time. She glanced up the track. And stopped.

A small figure had just jumped down from the wall. It began to walk slowly towards her, head down, hands in pockets, round the puddles, over the stones. The girl stared, she cried, she threw back her head and yelled, 'CLAIRE!'

The cry rang up the valley. The kestrel on his last sortie heard it and tensed. Rabbits venturing out in the fields heard it and froze. Claire heard it, looked up and saw the tall, thin figure down the track.

'Jakey,' she said and then she began to run.

MOY McCRORY

The Application Form

'It's arrived, it's arrived! Wake up you lazy . . .!'

Nell pounded her sleeping son, reaching across him as he lay in bed to draw the thin curtains and let more of the bright morning sun flood into his untidy room. A pair of red eyes that were still heavy with sleep stared out from under the blankets hating her. As they gradually focused, their attention was directed not at her but at the brown envelope being waved in front of them. Sleepily Brendan took it from her and put it down on the table. He threw back the covers and got slowly to his feet, looking unsteady and vaguely stupid in his striped pyjamas.

'Well go on! Open it!'

'Oh God . . . in a minute,' he answered dully, stumbling out of the room towards the lavatory. 'Christ!' he blasphemed as he drew the catch.

Nell's face piqued. She had annoyed him with her enthusiasm and now she felt as if she had acted improperly as she waited lamely for him to come back. He felt rotten, but his mother should have learnt that he was always irritable in the morning, she should have known better than to expect anything from him, he always woke up badly.

Back in his room he attempted a grin, but it was more of a

grimace than anything else. His mouth tasted stale and he wished that she would go instead of standing awkwardly by the side of the bed, reminding him with her dejected figure that he had taken the edge off her happiness.

The letter was a formality, for when Brendan's results had arrived they had known that he would be going to Queen's. And there it was, the definite confirmation of his place. All that day Nell walked about in a daze. Her son, going to University! No one in her family had ever done that before. She phoned her sisters and, wanting to tell yet more people, made an unnecessary trip to the shops to drop into the conversation with her best English telephone voice:

'Of course, Brendan's going to the University this Autumn yooneow,' drawing out the words to make the sentence last as long as possible. 'The' university, because Nell thought there was only one.

'What's he going to do there?' Mrs Carmichael asked with a look of disgust. She had either misheard or believed that university was a type of borstal.

Nell thought for a moment. What would he do? More schoolwork? She had never thought to ask him and she did not have the vaguest idea how the university functioned. She felt rather foolish as she mumbled that he would 'learn things'. It suddenly sounded rather pointless.

'But like what?' Mrs Carmichael asked. 'I mean . . . what sort of things? Hasn't he learnt enough already?'

Nell could see that she was not going to be fobbed off so easily. Sod her, she cursed inwardly. Why did someone always have to be so damned bloody clever?

'Oh, they learn all sorts of things nowadays, you know, yooneow . . .' She was struggling and the other woman knew it.

'No, I don't. I can't imagine why anyone has to stay on at school all the time they do now. I was out working when I was fourteen, I'd learnt all they had to teach me by then, me studying was over. What they're filling their heads up with now I can't guess. Sitting at desks like big kids when they could be out earning money.'

'Oh, but they don't look at it like that, they just go on learning. You can never get enough education it seems. When you've learned one thing there's always something else waiting to be studied.'

'Like what?'

God, but she was being awkward this morning. Nell could have kicked her but didn't want to give her the satisfaction of seeing her riled. 'Woodwork, philosophy, architecture, Russian . . .'

'Russian! What's the bloody good of learning that unless he's going to spy.'

Some of the other neighbours started to laugh.

'Is it like a school then this university?' one of them asked.

'I don't really know,' Nell admitted in a voice which was only a little flatter than usual. 'I expect it is. He'll have to read a lot I suppose.'

'Well I think it's wonderful, just wonderful,' Mr Maguire said nodding with approval. 'And I think we can all be grateful that a fine young man like Brendan is prepared to sacrifice his life to help others.'

Nell stared at him queerly.

'Tell me,' he said turning to her. 'When he comes out does he go straight into the priesthood, or do they send him away to the missions for further training? I mean, is he fully qualified, or does he have to do a bit of practical work first?'

'Och Maguire, you've got it wrong again,' Mrs Carmichael growled. 'He's going to university, not a bloody seminary.'

'Well, well,' Mr Maguire said, not one to be easily dismayed, 'I always said he'd turn out well.'

'But what will he do when he finishes?' Old Mrs Daly asked.

'That's a point . . .' said Mrs Carmichael turning to Nell. 'What will he do love, you know, when he's finished?'

'He'll get a good job.'

Nell never doubted that this education Brendan was about to receive would fail to unlock the door to a successful life ever after. But the neighbours looked uneasily at each other.

'How long does it take then?'

'Three years, or more if he decides to go on even further.'

They drew in their breath. 'God, but that's a long time. Better get his name down for the Post Office.'

Eileen was genuinely pleased for her brother when she heard the news. She felt saddened too, because it meant that he would be leaving home, and she would miss him. They had always been good friends, always been close. She was also a bit scared by the prospect because she knew what it would mean. Brendan would not live with them again as part of the family. He would only ever return as a visitor, from the moment he left to embark on his university career. He would no longer be tied by his father's dominance and stubborn authority. He would be free of it, and Eileen knew that that fact alone would change Brendan. He would not be the brother she needed in adversity.

Still, she found consolation thinking that it would only be a matter of two years before she could expect to do the same. If it was possible. Her father had already threatened to bring her out of school when she finished her 'O' levels, but he had not carried out his threat. She was going back that September to the sixth form. But she knew that he was not above changing his mind and so the prospect hung over her like a dark cloud. But she had worked out a solution, if it became necessary. She would leave home at eighteen anyway. There was nothing he could do about that. She would pack a bag and get out. He could not stop her. But she was worried by the next two years without Brendan to back her up. She felt indebted to her brother, because just having someone older than her meant that she had extra time to work things out. She was legacee to Brendan's problems.

When Brendan began to question their faith at the age of sixteen, Eileen was there to experience those doubts with him. By the time she reached that age herself she had already had two years to sort out the same problems. It was as if being two years younger enabled her to develop a better understanding when she reached that same age. It was, she was sure, the only single advantage that she had over him. She was always the more decisive of the two, clearer in her ideas than he was. All their relatives commented on it, that she seemed to understand things. She did. She understood that to her parents Brendan was really the only one that mattered. Her understanding did not spare her any pain, but increased it.

When Brendan spoke her parents listened, especially her mother. Sometimes it almost drove her mad to see her mother being weighed down by Brendan's adolescent authority. But she could not blame her brother for that. It saddened her to think that he might go through life believing in this power vested from God that all men possessed. He might end up like their father.

'I give the orders in this house!' their father would yell and his wife, standing behind her husband, would nod meekly and agree, only right and fitting.

Eileen had spotted the warning signs, for Brendan was beginning to show that annoying arrogance he had first displayed at fourteen when Eileen had hated him. He came home from the Irish Christian Brothers' School one day saying, 'What have women ever done? Our physics teacher said women were just the tools of men and that it is our Christian duty not to take advantage of their natural inferiority, because He has made it like that for a purpose. Tools,' he repeated staring dreamily out of the window.

Eileen had felt destroyed. She cried in bed not wanting to be merely a tool. It was so unfair, she could not even be an altar boy. And now again at eighteen he was lording it over his mother, treating her as though she was an idiot. Eileen hated seeing him behave like that. It drove her crazy.

'Make us a cup of tea,' he'd say and Nell would shoot out into the kitchen or, worse still, look up at Eileen and say 'well?' nodding towards the kitchen, because her son had made a request and it was right that the daughter should comply. She knew that if she had sat in a chair giving orders she would be told to get it herself, and called every name imaginable. If it came from Brendan it was authority, but if it came from her it was just cheek. Eileen never budged.

Nell could have clouted her. She wondered what was wrong with the girl lately. Didn't she see that she was worked to death? She had just come in and put the shopping down on the table and had to rush out to make tea. But Eileen never thought of offering, not that one, she'd just sit there and ignore everyone. Then she would get up and make herself a cup of tea, without thinking about anyone else. Bloody selfish that's what she was. The last few days in particular she had been getting on Nell's nerves. Sitting there without saying anything, leaving the room whenever she came in. Jealous, that's what it was. She was jealous of Brendan because Brendan was clever.

As she thought of her son a flush of happiness spread across her face. She sorted in the bag for the chocolate biscuits she'd bought especially. She'd take him one with his tea. She had never understood Eileen. She was temperamental, always had been. Even as a baby she had done the most crying. She had not been as lovable as Brendan. Nell imagined him as he had been, chuckling away, playing with a rattle and felt a gag in her throat thinking how quickly her son had grown up. Here he was about to go to university. She remembered his first day at school. He had held her hand nervously going up the road. But he had not given any trouble, settling in behind a desk and starting to play with some coloured counters that he found. He hadn't even seen her leave, so absorbed he was. She had come home and cried. It was funny to think of that. But Eileen now, she wasn't at all like Brendan, not easy. Last night for instance, he had only remarked that there was no sugar in his tea and she had hit the roof. Told him to get up and get it himself and called him all sorts of names.

She had had to intervene.

'For God's sake stop arguing!' she had shouted. She hated rows between the kids. She had enough to put up with from her husband without those two following suit.

'Get the sugar bowl, Eileen,' she told the girl and what did she do? She let loose a torrent of abuse at poor Brendan's head *and* half the sugar lumps! They went all over the floor. It was a good job their father wasn't there, he'd have killed them. She had a temper that one. God, life certainly was never boring with her around! Nell found herself grinning despite herself. Really it was something she had long wanted to do herself, chuck something at her husband. But it would have to be something a bit more weighty if it was to make any impression on his thick skull, she thought – the kettle, or the coal bucket. But poor Brendan, it was quite comical really. She went back into the living room smiling.

'This came with the afternoon post,' Brendan said fishing a green application form out of his trouser pocket. 'It's for the grant. I've already been down to the education offices and checked, I should qualify for the maximum.'

'Just as bloody well you do,' Nell said sipping her tea, 'because we couldn't afford to keep you.'

'No. Indeed. That is why I, that is, your son, will get a maximum grant . . .' Brendan explained with deliberate slowness as if talking to someone with difficulty understanding.

Eileen glared at him. 'Just cut out the comedy, smart lad.'

'Oh God, not you again!' Nell said turning to her daughter. 'What's wrong with you now?'

'He knows,' she said sullenly sinking back into her chair.

Brendan continued as if nothing had happened.

'The thing is, father has to fill out some bits, but it's straightforward enough. The sooner he does it, the sooner I'll know for sure what I have to live on next year.'

His mother nodded. She did not ask to see the forms. Why should she? To the water, gas and electricity boards she did not exist. Her name never appeared on any official documents. Whenever brown manilla envelopes with little windows cut out in them came through the door she ignored them, for she had learnt that they were not her concern. It was only her husband who was requested to fill in forms, that was just the way it was and she no longer even had curiosity to see them.

'Show them to your father when he gets home tonight. With a bit of luck you could have them ready and back in the office by tomorrow.'

'I've already filled in the bits I can: dates of birth, other dependent children and all that. So all he has to do is the part about income.'

It was straighforward enough, even rather simple. There should not have been any problems.

'I'm not filling that bloody thing in, and that's final!' His father's voice was harsh. He was beginning to yell. His face was obstinate, the chin stubborn and the mouth set. Brendan expected him to stamp his foot.

He knew that look on his father's face too well. Whenever he had to stick his tongue into his cheek as he was doing now it was a sure sign that he was in his fixed position. Putting his tongue in his cheek was a device he used to stop himself spluttering, which was undignified. It was always accompanied by speeded-up breathing, and a flush of irritation as he became more irrational and heated. Brendan knew that there was no point arguing with his father when he had reached that stage, but he thought he might be able to explain the consequences of his father's reaction and in this way alter the course of threatened events.

'But if you don't fill it in, I can't get a grant, and if I can't get a grant I can't go to university,' he explained tiredly. It was a weariness borne of knowledge of his father's intractable nature.

'For God's sake,' Nell said, 'why can't you just fill the thing in. What harm is there?'

'Harm!' he screamed, 'Harm! You expect me to tell everyone what I earn! Some tuppenny-hapenny office clerk knowing how much I bring home every week? I'm not filling that in and that's an end to it. You're entitled to a grant. They'll have to give it to you.'

'Not unless you fill in the form. They won't take my word for it. Any one could go down there and say that their parents can't support them. They need to know how much you earn in order to make an accurate assessment; unless you are suggesting that you would rather pay for me, that is, that you are able to.' Brendan's voice was mocking.

'Go to Hell!' his father shouted, striking out blindly with his fist and winding his son in the belly. He had started panting, the look he gave his son was of hate. He despised the young buck, daring to suggest that he didn't earn enough. Let him try to earn his own living. Let's see who does the best at it.

'Go and work in bloody Ford's,' he spat.

Brendan sank back, tears beginning to well up. Don't cry in front of him. Don't let him see that you're upset. Weak, a weakling, mummy's boy. Insults smarted in his head. So that was it, his father's plan for him. Work in Ford's. Don't dare dream of getting away from that. It was good enough for him so it must be good enough for the son . . .

'Bullies are cowards,' his mother always told him whenever he got into trouble at school. 'Stand up to them and they go away.'

But this time it was not so simple. Brendan was powerless while his father triumphed in the display of his control over the boy's life.

He remembered the first time that he had stood up to his father's temper. It was just a little over a year ago. Eileen was not quite fifteen. She was skinny and her hair was still in plaits then. He did not mind his father knocking him about, but he could not bear to see him hitting Eileen. It wasn't fair. Even if repetition meant that it had become commonplace and to some extent the girl was used to it, it still didn't seem right to Brendan. He remembered the look of horror and surprise on her face when he had stood between her and their father. Behind him his father was still striking out with blows. It took him a while to register that it was no longer his daughter but Brendan's back that the fists were striking.

'The little slut! The little bitch! Lady bloody muck!'

All Brendan had wanted to do was cover his sister's ears so that she would not hear any more insults. That was all he really intended. But once between them, he had swung round and landed a punch squarely in his father's mouth. He couldn't remember who had been the most surprised. But it was the quickest solution to stop him shouting. Thank God their mother had not been there. Nothing was ever said about it after. Their father pretended that it had not happened. But Brendan saw how he was less quick to hit Eileen after that.

He looked over now and saw his sister. She looked terrifying. She was white, completely white, the colour had drained out of her while she had listened to her father telling Brendan that he was still the one who gave the orders. Her father's temper stirred the hatred in the girl. Right then she hated him with every inch of her wiry frame. She wanted to throw herself at him, beat him to blood pulp with her own small fists. Beat and beat until the life went out of him. She despised him for dredging up such violence from her when it should have lain deep and forgotten. Eileen was terrified by her emotions. She knew that at times like this she had anger enough to kill and she retched, disgusted with herself.

Nell was crying. Why did they always have to be arguing? Why couldn't they be like other families? All she wanted was some peace. A quiet life. Hadn't she worked hard all her life and got nothing easy? Hadn't she earned some rest? And this morning she had been so proud, proud enough for the whole street. She had felt as if she would burst until she told everyone her news. And now her husband had destroyed that feeling.

The pen lay on the table, the green application form next to it. All he had to do was to pick it up and sign it. If it was up to her, she would sign it. What possible difference could it make? She remembered the means test as a child. The men in grey overcoats standing in their kitchen. Looking at everything, assessing, making values, telling her mother what she ought to sell. Nell couldn't understand what right they had to come into their home, but she was only a child then. How was it possible? These strangers came and put a price on everything. Her mother's head had hung down, sobbing.

'You've still got a table!' they told her roughly.

They went authoritatively into rooms opening cupboards, investigating.

'What are they looking for Mam?' she asked.

'Hush. Nothing, nothing. I'm a woman on my own. I've no man now,' was all her mother ever said.

'Sell those ornaments,' they commanded. There was no room for attachments, or sentiment. They were poor now.

'Those rings on your finger, are they gold?'

'Please, please, Dear God,' Nell prayed, 'grant my son the chance I never had, Mother Mary I beg of you.' She looked at the pen, it lay resolutely on the table.

Eileen was trying to catch her mother's attention. She waved her arms noiselessly from the kitchen door.

'What in God's name is wrong with that girl,' she thought. Fancy choosing now of all times to make them all tea! But over the hiss of the boiling kettle Eileen whispered conspiratorially:

'Why don't you fill it in – tomorrow, when he's at work?' She nodded in her father's direction. On the other side of the wall the image of her husband burned in Nell's eyes.

'Oh God no, I can't,' she whispered.

'Why not?' the daughter persisted. 'I'll forge his signature! It's simple – they won't bother to check and he need never know.'

'It's not that!' Oh, if only things could be so simple, she thought, suddenly feeling old and tired. 'It's not that at all. But I don't know . . .'

She hesitated, dreading her daughter's clear gaze.

'I mean . . . I don't know what he earns, he's never told me.'
Eileen's mouth opened as if to say something, then closed
again. The girl looked stunned.

'Well, a man's got to have his little bit of self-respect,' Nell
carried on, but it sounded hollow. She felt irritated. The girl was
young yet, she would learn. She would come to see how things
had to be a certain way, how things were done.

'Well you know,' she continued, 'It's always been like that.'
Eileen wasn't listening. She was sobbing gently over the tray.
Nell was surprised. She felt a sudden overwhelming surge of love
for her daughter. Her own eyes began to prick with tears, seeing
her own child, the one who was always ready to fight back, to
hold her own, now hanging limply, the life gone out of her.

Nell picked up the tray and marched aggressively into the
living room. But her courage left her as soon as she saw him.
The cups rattled. She put the tray down and it rang like a bell
against the polished surface of the table. There was no other
sound. Keeping her hand steady she poured him a cup. He took
it from her without a word and began to slurp. Christ, he
irritated her sometimes! She looked around. Both Brendan and
Eileen had disappeared. She felt nervous. She poured herself a cup
of tea and raised it shakily to her lips, but she had no taste for it
and let it sink back onto the tray before she too left the room.

Something had to be done. Nell couldn't sleep that night –
or the next. There was no point arguing with him. The more he
was pushed, the more he resisted. She knew him too well. What
may have been over-reaction now became solid policy. If he
were to give in now, he would look weak, irresolute. So while
Brendan had pleaded, desperately, he had furthered no cause
other than his father's obstinacy.

That morning he had asked his father if he would consider
disowning him legally. He had found out that he wouldn't need
the signature if he was 'disinherited'. The word had made
Brendan laugh. What did he stand to inherit beyond his father's
name? His father's example?

He had sworn at Brendan, called him a bastard anyhow. 'I've
got no son! You're no son for me!' He stormed out of the room
after striking haphazardly at Brendan's head.

They were at stalemate: he refused to talk and, of course, he would not disown his son publicly. Nell could have told Brendan as much. What a scandal! So while he walked around pretending to have no son, playing a game of silence with him, ignoring him and looking past him and enjoying his own stubbornness, his ploy of 'let's see who cracks first!', he would not put his argument on solid ground. It was private. He wasn't going to have some clever-dick lawyer meddling in his business!

Nell lay in the dark listening to him breathing. God how he slept – with a clear conscience. She was tortured. She so desperately wanted her son to go to University. It was so near her grasp to be so cruelly wrenched away – and by her husband! There was no sense, no logic, in what was happening. What should have been a wonderful occasion had been changed to one of misery. Tears ran down her face. Why was he doing this to her? He was blighting his own son's life, nipping the bud before it flowered. When Brendan should have been given every chance to get on in life, she thought, how could he make his way in the world if his own father blocked him? To Nell it was a matter of utmost urgency. One day Brendan would have to support a family. Surely he would stand a better chance if he was educated. Why couldn't her husband see that?

'Jesus, send me guidance,' she implored.

At the first light she rose and blessed herself with holy water from the wall font. 'In the name of the Father and of the Son and of the Holy Ghost, Amen,' she recited mechanically.

She might have been the ghost, she thought ruefully as she caught sight of herself in the dressing-table mirror – the unheard, unseen, performing the sign of the cross. Why couldn't she sign the form? Why did it have to be their father? 'Father! Father! Bloody father!' she cursed, but an idea began to form. While she knew that she was powerless to make him listen, she did know that there was somebody else, somebody whom she would only have to threaten him with.

The following Saturday she came home with her shopping basket and laid it squarely on the kitchen table in front of him.

'The price of butter's gone up. And cat food! Look at this,' she said piling tins up in a pyramid and pointing to the price labels. 'We'll have to shoot the cat next!'

The ginger tom looked up at her, then put its head between its

Stepping Out

paws and continued to sleep. The newspaper rustled slightly.
From behind it her husband mumbled something.

'I called in on Father Gallghan . . .' she continued brightly,
hoping her anxiety would not show, 'to ask for advice.'

Had her voice suddenly grown louder? She must try to keep it
even.

'I thought that he might be able to help us. About Brendan.'

'What!' He laid his paper to one side and stared at her.

'Well,' she said, trying not to flinch. 'I just thought that he
might know a way of getting round those forms. You know . . .
I mean . . . maybe he could sign them for us and vouch that we
can't afford to keep Brendan at University. They would have to
accept the word of a priest, wouldn't they?'

His mouth dropped open.

'I only explained to him how difficult it was . . . I mean, it is,
isn't it?'

She tried to sound as if she was in agreement.

'I don't know what you earn, so I can't fill it in.'

'You told the priest that!'

'Well of course. I had to explain the situation. I must say, he
did seem rather surprised. He kept saying that he had always
found you to be reasonable before . . . funny that, isn't it?' She
hoped she sounded guileless. 'I mean, you said yourself that
they had no right to ask you such things. I explained that you
were refusing on the grounds of privacy . . .' but she looked
acutely embarrassed . . . 'it's nothing to be ashamed of, you said
so yourself.'

'I'm ashamed all right!' he yelled. 'I'm ashamed of my bloody
wife! That she could be so damned stupid!'

Nell winced as if she had been struck. This was what she was
most scared of. She had to remain cool and not shout back, for
if she lost her temper she might tell him the truth – that she was
too ashamed to speak to anyone about it. She could not have
endured the pity from her neighbours, pity for being married to
such an oaf. She kept him secret for her own self-respect.

'Anyway, Father Gallghan said that he would come round to
have a quiet word with you . . . he'll probably sign the forms
then.' She tried to sound as if she really believed it.

'You stupid cow! By Christ. I'll kill you!' His face was pink.

'Whatever is wrong?'

'Do you always go blabbing to the bloody priest, letting him know all our business? What are you, a total moron?'

Nell looked at him straight. 'I always tell the priest ... everything.'

He had never struck her. He thought she ought to be grateful. He was a model husband because he did not beat his wife. The kids ... well, that was discipline. God, he didn't want to see the priest now!

'Get me those forms!' he ordered. He would sign the things and have done with it. 'And you can tell the priest it was a false alarm!'

He'd fix it. Tell him his silly wife had made a mistake – 'Ha, ha, you know Father, ha, ha, women ...' that would do it.

Upstairs Eileen was jumping and hugging her brother who held the green form ready to go into an envelope. His future was sealed.

'Come and live with me when you're eighteen,' he said. 'Then you will be a legal entity. Dad won't be able to mess you around.'

Brendan knew that she would have a harder time of it. He put his arms round her wanting to offer support. She felt steel-framed and angular. He felt her hesitate a moment, as if she would push him away. His sister needed no one, he had always been a little in awe of her resolve. She had an ability to go out and get things done on her own. She did not need the approval of others that he so desperately sought. Now he needed her. He wanted to know that he could help her and that she would not reject him. Eileen did not blame her brother. 'You'll face this in two years, only mam won't support you like she has me you know.'

She knew. She had learnt it long ago. She softened and they both cried onto each other's shoulders as they had when they were small and used to fight and stop to make friends, each sobbing with fear that the other would not want to.

Downstairs their mother was giving thanks in front of the statue of Our Lady.

'In the name of the Father and of the Son,' she began without the slightest trace of irony.

Personal Essay
by Moy McCrory

To explain any of my writing I find it useful to state that I was born into an Irish Catholic family. You might wonder what relevance, if any, this single biographical fact has. Why should I include it in a discussion about the act of writing?

Although I was born and brought up in England, the traditions of my family were not typically English and in my case, short stories were a natural progression out of a childhood of Irish storytelling. They are direct descendants from the myths and sagas recounted by Bards and storytellers (seanchaí) who travelled from place to place speaking wondrous tales. In the days before television, radio and readily available books, speaking was a means of keeping history alive. If we look earlier still, before the development of reading and writing it was the only means of recording it. To be a poet and singer (as the Bard was chiefly) was an important job, as necessary to daily life as an engineer is today. The history carried in poems, songs and stories of the seanchaí brought news of battles, of gains and losses and of social change. Stories were the repository of memory of a civilisation on the brink of literacy. Obviously the more entertaining a story was the less chance it had of being forgotten.

To me, every short story that I write belongs in a cultural framework which is why I tend to group my stories into collections. Because of their form they can be viewed separately but if someone were to look at more than one of my stories they would discover a connection. Just as the Bards told of their successive battles, each one unique but interdependent upon a common aim, there is a common identity running throughout my tales.

I inherited a broad range of imagery due to my family's catholicism, and with it the humour of working people struggling to survive with spirit and wit. I choose the word 'struggling' to describe them because their daily existence was not easy. I use humour in much of my writing to show how the adults I grew up among needed to laugh; they laughed to keep up their morale in difficult circumstances and it is their identity which is stamped on my writing. Even when I do not directly write about them, the influence remains because I developed my ideas out of the same experience and background.

What I write about are often those things about growing up where I was not in accordance with those around me. Imagine how good that feels; writing down everything you would criticise and putting it into a story to let people know how unfair they were. Sometimes it feels like getting your own back!

88

Now let us look at words – for what would any writer be without them? Here again that biographical fact surfaces when I say that I consider myself fortunate. I have the flexibility of the English language which I studied at school, to be used and delighted in, and I have the polyglot of my family who spoke using Irish idioms through English. Lastly I have a rich gaelic culture complete with a separate language that I occasionally borrow from. I mine these resources like a vein of the purest gold, for these are the raw materials I make use of in order to write.

In 'The Application Form' my intention was to hold up to the reader certain attitudes which pass as 'normal' in our society which invests more power in men than in women. I did not set out to show how everything can be put right by, for example, all following the same set of beliefs. My aim was just to let the reader see how certain values when swallowed wholesale can be acted out unthinkingly on other people in ways which are simply not fair.

It is an injustice in the story that the brother and sister should be treated differently if the grounds for such selective treatment are based on gender. The parents in the story feel that Brendan is important while Eileen is not listened to and hardly ever taken seriously. It is as if the parents are saying that her life will never be as valuable as the boy's. Why? If it was because of some individual behaviour then maybe there would be a reason to favour one over the other, but it would be favouritism earned on merit. In this story the attitudes of the parents are based on feelings about gender which both of them have absorbed from a society that does not treat women as equals.

I do not blame the parents for holding values which they have never thought to question, but by writing about the effects of such beliefs I hope to show the unfairness of such general assumptions. It is important that the father in this story is the head of the Catholic household, for the Catholic Church does not give women equal status with men. Catholic women cannot become priests and are prevented from performing the sacraments. This is a contributory factor to the father's feelings of superiority, rather than equality with women. He senses that his authority is slipping, and in his case I show authority to be unjustified because he does not use it wisely for the common good but irresponsibly to maintain whatever slight feeling of power he has at home. As he abuses his authority Eileen loses all respect for him; the more he argues the more she feels contempt. It should be clear that he has no real authority over her or Brendan.

If Eileen feels the unfairness of her parents' behaviour because she is at the receiving end of it much of the time, Brendan, having to struggle against his father's intolerable behaviour on this occasion, may stand a better chance of understanding it as a result. Hopefully he will not grow into the kind of man his father is, and he may learn to use his maleness in a way that is not oppressive.

These attitudes are very deep within us. Nell, who succeeded in tricking her 'oafish husband' into signing the form, does not think about the values which have promoted such a situation. In fact she returns to them. She thanks God whom she loves and knows is superior. She has also learnt from institutional religion that God is male. When she prays automatically and without thinking she unwittingly gives voice to the idea that a woman can only be a secondary human. That is the tragedy, the irony, and I hope, the bit that makes people think.

NADINE GORDIMER

A Chip of Glass Ruby

When the duplicating machine was brought into the house, Bamjee said, 'Isn't it enough that you've got the Indians' troubles on your back?' Mrs Bamjee said, with a smile that showed the gap of a missing tooth but was confident all the same, 'What's the difference, Yusuf? We've all got the same troubles.'

'Don't tell me that. We don't have to carry passes; let the natives protest against passes on their own, there are millions of them. Let them go ahead with it.'

The nine Bamjee and Pahad children were present at this exchange as they were always; in the small house that held them all there was no room for privacy for the discussion of matters they were too young to hear, and so they had never been too young to hear anything. Only their sister and half-sister, Girlie, was missing; she was the eldest, and married. The children looked expectantly, unalarmed and interested, at Bamjee, who had neither left the room nor settled down again to the task of rolling his own cigarettes, which had been interrupted by the arrival of the duplicator. He had looked at the thing that had come hidden in a wash-basket and conveyed in a black man's taxi, and the children turned on it too, their eyes surrounded by thick lashes like those still, open flowers with hairy tentacles that close on whatever touches them.

91

'A fine thing to have on the table where we eat,' was all he said at last. They smelled the machine among them; a smell of cold black grease. He went out, heavily on tiptoe, in his troubled way.

'It's going to go nicely on the sideboard!' Mrs Bamjee was busy making a place by removing the two pink glass vases filled with plastic carnations and the hand-painted velvet runner with the picture of the Taj Mahal.

After supper she began to run off leaflets on the machine. The family lived in that room – the three other rooms in the house were full of beds – and they were all there. The older children shared a bottle of ink while they did their homework, and the two little ones pushed a couple of empty milk-bottles in and out the chair-legs. The three-year-old fell asleep and was carted away by one of the girls. They all drifted off to bed eventually; Bamjee himself went before the older children – he was a fruit-and-vegetable hawker and was up at half past four every morning to get to the market by five. 'Not long now,' said Mrs Bamjee. The older children looked up and smiled at him. He turned his back on her. She still wore the traditional clothing of a Moslem woman, and her body, which was scraggy and unimportant as a dress on a peg when it was not host to a child, was wrapped in the trailing rags of a cheap sari and her thin black plait was greased. When she was a girl, in the Transvaal town where they lived still, her mother fixed a chip of glass ruby in her nostril; but she had abandoned that adornment as too old-style, even for her, long ago.

She was up until long after midnight, turning out leaflets. She did it as if she might have been pounding chillies.

Bamjee did not have to ask what the leaflets were. He had read the papers. All the past week Africans had been destroying their passes and then presenting themselves for arrest. Their leaders were jailed on charges of incitement, campaign offices were raided – someone must be helping the few minor leaders who were left to keep the campaign going without offices or equipment. What was it the leaflets would say – 'Don't go to work tomorrow', 'Day of Protest', 'Burn Your Pass for Freedom'? He didn't want to see.

He was used to coming home and finding his wife sitting at

the table deep in discussion with strangers or people whose names were familiar by repute. Some were prominent Indians, like the lawyer, Dr Abdul Mohammed Khan, or the big business-man, Mr Moonsamy Patel, and he was flattered, in a suspicious way, to meet them in his house. As he came home from work next day he met Dr Khan coming out of the house and Dr Khan – a highly educated man – said to him, 'A wonderful woman.' But Bamjee had never caught his wife out in any presumption; she behaved properly, as any Moslem woman should, and once her business with such gentlemen was over would never, for instance, have sat down to eat with them. He found her now back in the kitchen, setting about the preparation of dinner and carrying on a conversation on several different wave-lengths with the children. 'It's really a shame if you're tired of lentils, Jimmy, because that's what you're getting – Amina, hurry up, get a pot of water going – don't worry, I'll mend that in a minute, just bring the yellow cotton, and there's a needle in the cigarette box on the sideboard.'

'Was that Dr Khan leaving?' said Bamjee.

'Yes, there's going to be a stay-at-home on Monday. Desai's ill, and he's got to get the word around by himself. Bob Jali was up all night printing leaflets, but he's gone to have a tooth out.' She had always treated Bamjee as if it were only a mannerism that made him appear uninterested in politics, the way some woman will persist in interpreting her husband's bad temper as an endearing gruffness hiding boundless goodwill, and she talked to him of these things just as she passed on to him neighbours' or family gossip.

'What for do you want to get mixed up with these killings and stonings and I don't know what? Congress should keep out of it. Isn't it enough with the Group Areas?'

She laughed. 'Now, Yusuf, you know you don't believe that. Look how you said the same thing when the Group Areas started in Natal. You said we should begin to worry when we get moved out of our own houses here in the Transvaal. And then your own mother lost her house in Noorddorp, and there you are; you saw that nobody's safe. Oh, Girlie was here this afternoon, she says Ismail's brother's engaged – that's nice, isn't it? His mother will be pleased; she was worried.'

'Why was she worried?' asked Jimmy, who was fifteen, and old enough to patronise his mother.

'Well, she wanted to see him settled. There's a party on Sunday week at Ismail's place – you'd better give me your suit to give to the cleaners tomorrow, Yusuf.'

One of the girls presented herself at once. 'I'll have nothing to wear, Ma.'

Mrs Bamjee scratched her sallow face. 'Perhaps Girlie will lend you her pink, eh? Run over to Girlie's place now and say I say will she lend it to you.'

The sound of commonplaces often does service as security, and Bamjee, going to sit in the armchair with the shiny armrests that was wedged between the table and the sideboard, lapsed into an unthinking doze that, like all times of dreamlike ordinariness during those weeks, was filled with uneasy jerks and starts back into reality. The next morning, as soon as he got to market, he heard that Dr Khan had been arrested. But that night Mrs Bamjee sat up making a new dress for her daughter; the sight disarmed Bamjee, reassured him again, against his will, so that the resentment he had been making ready all day faded into a morose and accusing silence. Heaven knew, of course, who came and went in the house during the day. Twice in that week of riots, raids and arrests, he found black women in the house when he came home; plain ordinary native women in doeks, drinking tea. This was not a thing other Indian women would have in their homes, he thought bitterly; but then his wife was not like other people, in a way he could not put his finger on, except to say what it was not: not scandalous, not punishable, not rebellious. It was, like the attraction that had led him to marry her, Pahad's widow with five children, something he could not see clearly.

When the Special Branch knocked steadily on the door in the small hours of Thursday morning he did not wake up, for his return to consciousness was always set in his mind to half past four, and that was more than an hour away. Mrs Bamjee got up herself, struggled into Jimmy's raincoat which was hanging over a chair and went to the front door. The clock on the wall – a wedding present when she married Pahad – showed three o'clock when she snapped on the light, and she knew at once who it was on the other side of the door. Although she was not surprised, her hands shook like a very old person's as she undid the locks and the complicated catch on the wire burglar-proofing. And then she opened the door and they were there – two coloured policemen in plain clothes. 'Zanip Bamjee?'

'Yes.'

As they talked, Bamjee woke up in the sudden terror of having overslept. Then he became conscious of men's voices. He heaved himself out of bed in the dark and went to the window, which, like the front door, was covered with a heavy mesh of thick wire against intruders from the dingy lane it looked upon. Bewildered, he appeared in the room, where the policemen were searching through a soapbox of papers beside the duplicating machine. 'Yusuf, it's for me,' Mrs Bamjee said.

At once, the snap of a trap, realisation came. He stood there in an old shirt before the two policemen, and the woman was going off to prison because of the natives. 'There you are!' he shouted, standing away from her. 'That's what you've got for it. Didn't I tell you? Didn't I? That's the end of it now. That's the finish. That's what it's come to.' She listened with her head at the slightest tilt to one side, as if to ward off a blow, or in compassion.

Jimmy, Pahad's son, appeared at the door with a suitcase; two or three of the girls were behind him. 'Here, Ma, you take my green jersey.' 'I've found your clean blouse.' Bamjee had to keep moving out of their way as they helped their mother to make ready. It was like the preparation for one of the family festivals his wife made such a fuss over; wherever he put himself, they bumped into him. Even the two policemen mumbled, 'Excuse me,' and pushed past into the rest of the house to continue their search. They took with them a tome that Nehru had written in prison; it had been bought from a persevering travelling salesman and kept, for years, on the mantelpiece. 'Oh, don't take that, please,' Mrs Bamjee said suddenly, clinging to the arm of the man who had picked it up.

The man held it away from her.

'What does it matter, Ma?'

It was true that no one in the house had ever read it; but she said, 'It's for my children.'

'Ma, leave it.' Jimmy, who was squat and plump, looked like a merchant advising a client against a roll of silk she had set her heart on. She went into the bedroom and got dressed. When she came out in her old yellow sari with a brown coat over it, the faces of the children were behind her like faces on the platform of a railway station. They kissed her goodbye. The policemen did not hurry her, but she seemed to be in a hurry just the same.

'What am I going to do?' Bamjee accused them all.

The policemen looked away patiently.

'It'll be all right. Girlie will help. The big children can manage. And Yusuf —' The children crowded in around her; two of the younger ones had awakened and appeared, asking shrill questions.

'Come on,' said the policemen.

'I want to speak to my husband.' She broke away and came back to him, and the movement of her sari hid them from the rest of the room for a moment. His face hardened in suspicious anticipation against the request to give some message to the next fool who would take up her pamphleteering until he, too, was arrested. 'On Sunday,' she said. 'Take them on Sunday.' He did not know what she was talking about. 'The engagement party,' she whispered, low and urgent. 'They shouldn't miss it. Ismail will be offended.'

They listened to the car drive away. Jimmy bolted and barred the front door, and then at once opened it again; he put on the raincoat that his mother had taken off. 'Going to tell Girlie,' he said. The children went back to bed. Their father did not say a word to any of them; their talk, the crying of the younger ones and the argumentative voices of the older, went on in the bedrooms. He found himself alone; he felt the night all around him. And then he happened to meet the clock face and saw with a terrible sense of unfamiliarity that this was not the secret night but an hour he should have recognised: the time he always got up. He pulled on his trousers and his dirty white hawker's coat and wound his grey muffler up to the stubble on his chin and went to work.

The duplicating machine was gone from the sideboard. The policemen had taken it with them, along with the pamphlets

and the conference reports and the stack of old newspapers that
had collected on top of the wardrobe in the bedroom – not the
thick dailies of the white men but the thin, impermanent-looking
papers that spoke up, sometimes interrupted by suppression or
lack of money, for the rest. It was all gone. When he had
married her and moved in with her and her five children, into
what had been the Pahad and became the Bamjee house, he had
not recognised the humble, harmless and apparently useless
routine tasks – the minutes of meetings being written up on the
dining-room table at night, the government blue books that
were read while the latest baby was suckled, the employment of
the fingers of the older children in the fashioning of crinklepaper
Congress rosettes – as activity intended to move mountains.
For years and years he had not noticed it, and now it was gone.

The house was quiet. The children kept to their lairs, crowded
on the beds with the doors shut. He sat and looked at the
sideboard, where the plastic carnations and the mat with the
picture of the Taj Mahal were in place. For the first few weeks
he never spoke of her. There was the feeling, in the house, that
he had wept and raged at her, that boulders of reproach had
thundered down upon her absence, and yet he had said not one
word. He had not been to inquire where she was; Jimmy and
Girlie had gone to Mohammed Ebrahim, the lawyer, and when
he found out that their mother had been taken – when she was
arrested, at least – to a big prison in the next town, they had
stood about outside the big prison door for hours while they
waited to be told where she had been moved from there. At last
they had discovered that she was fifty miles away, in Pretoria.
Jimmy asked Bamjee for five shillings to help Girlie pay the train
fare to Pretoria, once she had been interviewed by the police
and had been given a permit to visit her mother; he put three
two-shilling pieces on the table for Jimmy to pick up, and the
boy, looking at him keenly, did not know whether the extra
shilling meant anything, or whether it was merely that Bamjee
had no change.

It was only when relations and neighbours came to the house
that Bamjee would suddenly begin to talk. He had never been so
expansive in his life as he was in the company of these visitors,
many of them come on a polite call rather in the nature of a visit

of condolence. 'Ah, yes, yes, you can see how I am – you can see what has been done to me. Nine children, and I am on the cart all day. I get home at seven or eight. What are you to do? What can people like us do?'

'Poor Mrs Bamjee. Such a kind lady.'

'Well, you see for yourself. They walk in here in the middle of the night and leave a houseful of children. I'm out on the cart all day, I've got a living to earn.' Standing about in his shirt sleeves, he became quite animated; he would call for the girls to bring fruit drinks for the visitors. When they were gone, it was as if he, who was orthodox if not devout and never drank liquor, had been drunk and abruptly sobered up; he looked dazed and could not have gone over in his mind what he had been saying. And as he cooled, the lump of resentment and wrongedness stopped his throat again.

Bamjee found one of the little boys the centre of a self-important group of championing brothers and sisters in the room one evening, 'They've been cruel to Ahmed.'

'What has he done?' said the father.

'Nothing! Nothing!' The little girl stood twisting her handkerchief excitedly.

An older one, thin as her mother, took over, silencing the others with a gesture of her skinny hand. 'They did it at school today. They made an example of him.'

'What is an example?' said Bamjee impatiently.

'The teacher made him come up and stand in front of the whole class, and he told them, "You see this boy? His mother's in jail because she likes the natives so much. She wanted the Indians to be the same as natives."'

'It's terrible,' he said. His hands fell to his sides. 'Did she ever think of this?'

'That's why Ma's *there*,' said Jimmy, putting aside his comic and emptying out his schoolbooks upon the table. 'That's all the kids need to know. Ma's there because things like this happen. Petersen's a coloured teacher, and it's his black blood that's brought him trouble all his life, I suppose. He hates anyone who says everybody's the same because that takes away from him his bit of whiteness that's all he's got. What d'you expect? It's nothing to make too much fuss about.'

'Of course, you are fifteen and you know everything,' Bamjee mumbled at him.

'I don't say that. But I know Ma, anyway.' The boy laughed.

There was a hunger strike among the political prisoners, and Bamjee could not bring himself to ask Girlie if her mother was starving herself too. He would not ask; and yet he saw in the young woman's face the gradual weakening of her mother. When the strike had gone on for nearly a week one of the elder children burst into tears at the table and could not eat. Bamjee pushed his own plate away in rage.

Sometimes he spoke out loud to himself while he was driving the vegetable lorry. 'What for?' Again and again: 'What for?' She was not a modern woman who cut her hair and wore short skirts. He had married a good plain Moslem woman who bore children and stamped her own chillies. He had a sudden vision of her at the duplicating machine, that night just before she was taken away, and he felt himself maddened, baffled and hopeless. He had become the ghost of a victim, hanging about the scene of a crime whose motive he could not understand and had not had time to learn.

The hunger strike at the prison went into the second week. Alone in the rattling cab of his lorry, he said things that he heard as if spoken by someone else, and his heart burned in fierce agreement with them. 'For a crowd of natives who'll smash our shops and kill us in our houses when their time comes.' 'She will starve herself to death there.' 'She will die there.' 'Devils who will burn and kill us.' He fell into bed each night like a stone, and dragged himself up in the mornings as a beast of burden is beaten to its feet.

One of these mornings, Girlie appeared very early, while he was wolfing bread and strong tea – alternate sensations of dry solidity and stinging heat – at the kitchen table. Her real name was Fatima, of course, but she had adopted the silly modern name along with the clothes of the young factory girls among whom she worked. She was expecting her first baby in a week or two, and her small face, her cut and curled hair and the sooty arches drawn over her eyebrows did not seem to belong to her thrust-out body under a clean smock. She wore mauve lipstick and was smiling her cocky little white girl's smile, foolish and bold, not like an Indian girl's at all.

'What's the matter?' he said.

She smiled again. 'Don't you know? I told Bobby he must get me up in time this morning. I wanted to be sure I wouldn't miss you today.'

'I don't know what you're talking about.'

She came over and put her arm up around his unwilling neck and kissed the grey bristles at the side of his mouth. 'Many happy returns! Don't you know it's your birthday?'

'No,' he said. 'I didn't know, didn't think –.' He broke the pause by swiftly picking up the bread and giving his attention desperately to eating and drinking. His mouth was busy, but his eyes looked at her, intensely black. She said nothing, but stood there with him. She would not speak, and at last he said, swallowing a piece of bread that tore at his throat as it went down, 'I don't remember these things.'

The girl nodded, the Woolworth baubles in her ears swinging. 'That's the first thing she told me when I saw her yesterday – don't forget it's Bajie's birthday tomorrow.'

He shrugged over it. 'It means a lot to children. But that's how she is. Whether it's one of the old cousins or the neighbour's grandmother, she always knows when the birthday is. What importance is my birthday, while she's sitting there in a prison? I don't understand how she can do the things she does when her mind is always full of woman's nonsense at the same time – that's what I don't understand with her.'

'Oh, but don't you see?' the girl said. 'It's because she doesn't want anybody to be left out. It's because she always remembers; remembers everything – people without somewhere to live, hungry kids, boys who can't get educated – remembers all the time. That's how Ma is.'

'Nobody else is like that.' It was half a complaint.

'No, nobody else,' said his stepdaughter.

She sat herself down at the table, resting her belly. He put his head in his hands. 'I'm getting old' – but he was overcome by something much more curious, by an answer. He knew why he had desired her, the ugly widow with five children; he knew what way it was in which she was not like the others; it was there, like the fact of the belly that lay between him and her daughter.

CHARLOTTE PERKINS GILMAN

Turned

In her soft-carpeted, thick-curtained, richly furnished chamber, Mrs Marroner lay sobbing on the wide, soft bed.

She sobbed bitterly, chokingly, despairingly; her shoulders heaved and shook convulsively; her hands were tight-clenched. She had forgotten her elaborate dress, the more elaborate bedcover; forgotten her dignity, her self-control, her pride. In her mind was an overwhelming, unbelievable horror, an immeasurable loss, a turbulent, struggling mass of emotion.

In her reserved, superior, Boston-bred life, she had never dreamed that it would be possible for her to feel so many things at once, and with such trampling intensity.

She tried to cool her feelings into thoughts; to stiffen them into words; to control herself – and could not. It brought vaguely to her mind an awful moment in the breakers at York Beach, one summer in girlhood when she had been swimming under water and could not find the top.

In her uncarpeted, thin-curtained, poorly furnished chamber on the top floor, Gerta Petersen lay sobbing on the narrow, hard bed.

She was of larger frame than her mistress, grandly built and strong; but all her proud young womanhood was prostrate now, convulsed with agony, dissolved in tears. She did not try to control herself. She wept for two.

If Mrs Marroner suffered more from the wreck and ruin of a longer love – perhaps a deeper one; if her tastes were finer, her ideals loftier; if she bore the pangs of bitter jealousy and outraged pride, Gerta had personal shame to meet, a hopeless future, and a looming present which filled her with unreasoning terror.

She had come like a meek young goddess into that perfectly ordered house, strong, beautiful, full of goodwill and eager obedience, but ignorant and childish – a girl of eighteen.

Mr Marroner had frankly admired her, and so had his wife. They discussed her visible perfections and as visible limitations with that perfect confidence which they had so long enjoyed. Mrs Marroner was not a jealous woman. She had never been jealous in her life – till now.

Gerta had stayed and learned their ways. They had both been fond of her. Even the cook was fond of her. She was what is called 'willing', was unusually teachable and plastic; and Mrs Marroner, with her early habits of giving instruction, tried to educate her somewhat.

'I never saw anyone so docile,' Mrs Marroner had often commented. 'It is perfection in a servant, but almost a defect in character. She is so helpless and confiding.'

She was precisely that: a tall, rosy-cheeked baby; rich womanhood without, helpless infancy within. Her braided wealth of dead-gold hair, her grave blue eyes, her mighty shoulders and long, firmly moulded limbs seemed those of a primal earth spirit; but she was only an ignorant child, with a child's weakness.

When Mr Marroner had to go abroad for his firm, unwillingly, hating to leave his wife, he had told her he felt quite safe to leave her in Gerta's hands – she would take care of her.

'Be good to your mistress, Gerta,' he told the girl that last morning at breakfast. 'I leave her to you to take care of. I shall be back in a month at latest.'

Then he turned, smiling, to his wife. 'And you must take care of Gerta, too,' he said. 'I expect you'll have her ready for college when I get back.'

This was seven months ago. Business had delayed him from week to week, from month to month. He wrote to his wife, long, loving, frequent letters, deeply regretting the delay, explaining how necessary, how profitable it was, congratulating her on the wide resources she had, her well-filled, well-balanced mind, her many interests.

'If I should be eliminated from your scheme of things, by any of those "acts of God" mentioned on the tickets, I do not feel that you would be an utter wreck,' he said. 'That is very comforting to me. Your life is so rich and wide that no one loss, even a great one, would wholly cripple you. But nothing of the sort is likely to happen, and I shall be home again in three weeks – if this thing gets settled. And you will be looking so lovely, with that eager light in your eyes and the changing flush I know so well – and love so well! My dear wife! We shall have to have a new honeymoon – other moons come every month, why shouldn't the mellifluous kind?'

He often asked after 'little Gerta', sometimes enclosed a picture postcard to her, joked his wife about her laborious efforts to educate 'the child', was so loving and merry and wise –

All this was racing through Mrs Marroner's mind as she lay there with the broad, hemstitched border of fine linen sheeting crushed and twisted in one hand, and the other holding a sodden handkerchief.

She had tried to teach Gerta, and had grown to love the patient, sweet-natured child, in spite of her dullness. At work with her hands, she was clever, if not quick, and could keep small accounts from week to week. But to the woman who held a Ph.D., who had been on the faculty of a college, it was like baby-tending.

Perhaps having no babies of her own made her love the big child the more, though the years between them were but fifteen.

To the girl she seemed quite old, of course; and her young heart was full of grateful affection for the patient care which made her feel so much at home in this new land.

And then she had noticed a shadow on the girl's bright face. She looked nervous, anxious, worried. When the bell rang, she seemed startled, and would rush hurriedly to the door. Her peals of frank laughter no longer rose from the area gate as she stood talking with the always admiring tradesmen.

Mrs Marroner had laboured long to teach her more reserve with men, and flattered herself that her words were at last effective. She suspected the girl of homesickness, which was denied. She suspected her of illness, which was denied also. At last she suspected her of something which could not be denied.

For a long time she refused to believe it, waiting. Then she had to believe it, but schooled herself to patience and understanding. 'The poor child,' she said. 'She is here without a mother – she is so foolish and yielding – I must not be too stern with her.' And she tried to win the girl's confidence with wise, kind words.

But Gerta had literally thrown herself at her feet and begged her with streaming tears not to turn her away. She would admit nothing, explain nothing, but frantically promised to work for Mrs Marroner as long as she lived – if only she would keep her.

Revolving the problem carefully in her mind, Mrs Marroner thought she would keep her, at least for the present. She tried to repress her sense of ingratitude in one she had so sincerely tried to help, and the cold, contemptuous anger she had always felt for such weakness.

'The thing to do now,' she said to herself, 'is to see her through this safely. The child's life should not be hurt any more than is unavoidable. I will ask Dr Bleet about it – what a comfort a woman doctor is! I'll stand by the poor, foolish thing till it's over, and then get her back to Sweden somehow with her baby. How they do come where they are not wanted – and don't come where they are wanted!' And Mrs Marroner, sitting alone in the quiet, spacious beauty of the house, almost envied Gerta.

Then came the deluge.

She had sent the girl out for needed air towards dark. The late mail came; she took it in herself. One letter for her – her husband's letter. She knew the postmark, the stamp, the kind of typewriting. She impulsively kissed it in the dim hall. No one would suspect Mrs Marroner of kissing her husband's letters –

but she did, often.

She looked over the others. One was for Gerta, and not from Sweden. It looked precisely like her own. This struck her as a little odd, but Mr Marroner had several times sent messages and cards to the girl. She laid the letter on the hall table and took hers to her room.

'My poor child,' it began. What letter of hers had been sad enough to warrant that?

'I am deeply concerned at the news you send.' What news to concern him had she written? 'You must bear it bravely, little girl. I shall be home soon, and will take care of you, of course. I hope there is not immediate anxiety – you do not say. Here is money, in case you need it. I expect to get home in a month at latest. If you have to go, be sure to leave your address at my office. Cheer up – be brave – I will take care of you.'

The letter was typewritten, which was not unusual. It was unsigned, which was unusual. It enclosed an American bill – fifty dollars. It did not seem in the least like any letter she had ever had from her husband, or any letter she could imagine him writing. But a strange, cold feeling was creeping over her, like a flood rising around a house.

She utterly refused to admit the ideas which began to bob and push about outside her mind, and to force themselves in. Yet under the pressure of these repudiated thoughts she went downstairs and brought up the other letter – the letter to Gerta. She laid them side by side on a smooth dark space on the table; marched to the piano and played, with stern precision, refusing to think, till the girl came back. When she came in, Mrs Marroner rose quietly and came to the table. 'Here is a letter for you,' she said.

The girl stepped forward eagerly, saw the two lying together there, hesitated, and looked at her mistress.

'Take yours, Gerta. Open it, please.'

The girl turned frightened eyes upon her.

'I want you to read it, here,' said Mrs Marroner.

'Oh, ma'am – No! Please don't make me!'

'Why not?'

There seemed to be no reason at hand, and Gerta flushed more deeply and opened her letter. It was long; it was evidently puzzling to her; it began 'My dear wife.' She read it slowly.

'Are you sure it is your letter?' asked Mrs Marroner. 'Is not this one yours? Is not that one – mine?'

She held out the other letter to her.

'It is a mistake,' Mrs Marroner went on, with a hard quietness. She had lost her social bearings somehow, lost her usual keen sense of the proper thing to do. This was not life; this was a nightmare.

'Do you not see? Your letter was put in my envelope and my letter was put in your envelope. Now we understand it.'

But poor Gerta had no antechamber to her mind, no trained forces to preserve order while agony entered. The thing swept over her, resistless, overwhelming, She cowered before the outraged wrath she expected; and from some hidden cavern that wrath arose and swept over her in pale flame.

'Go and pack your trunk,' said Mrs Marroner. 'You will leave my house tonight. Here is your money.'

She laid down the fifty-dollar bill. She put with it a month's wages. She had no shadow of pity for those anguished eyes, those tears which she heard drop on the floor.

'Go to your room and pack,' said Mrs Marroner. And Gerta, always obedient, went.

Then Mrs Marroner went to hers, and spent a time she never counted, lying on her face on the bed.

But the training of the twenty-eight years which had elapsed before her marriage; the life at college, both as student and teacher; the independent growth which she had made, formed a very different background for grief from that in Gerta's mind.

After a while Mrs Marroner arose. She administered to herself a hot bath, a cold shower, a vigorous rubbing. 'Now I can think,' she said.

First she regretted the sentence of instant banishment. She went upstairs to see if it had been carried out. Poor Gerta! The tempest of her agony had worked itself out at last as in a child, and left her sleeping, the pillow wet, the lips still grieving, a big sob shuddering itself off now and then.

Mrs Marroner stood and watched her, and as she watched she considered the helpless sweetness of the face; the defenceless unformed character; the docility and habit of obedience which made her so attractive – and so easily a victim. Also she thought of the mighty force which had swept over her; of the great process now working itself out through her; of how pitiful and futile seemed any resistance she might have made.

She softly returned to her own room, made up a little fire, and sat by it, ignoring her feelings now, as she had before ignored her thoughts.

Here were two women and a man. One woman was a wife: loving, trusting, affectionate. One was a servant: loving, trusting, affectionate – a young girl, an exile, a dependant; grateful for any kindness; untrained, uneducated, childish. She ought, of course, to have resisted temptation; but Mrs Marroner was wise enough to know how difficult temptation is to recognise when it comes in the guise of friendship and from a source one does not suspect.

Gerta might have done better in resisting the grocer's clerk; had, indeed, with Mrs Marroner's advice, resisted several. But where respect was due, how could she criticise? Where obedience was due, how could she refuse – with ignorance to hold her blinded – until too late?

As the older, wiser woman forced herself to understand and extenuate the girl's misdeed and foresee her ruined future, a new feeling rose in her heart, strong, clear, and overmastering: a sense of measureless condemnation for the man who had done this thing. He knew. He understood. He could fully foresee and measure the consequences of his act. He appreciated to the full the innocence, the ignorance, the grateful affection, the habitual docility, of which he deliberately took advantage.

Mrs Marroner rose to icy peaks of intellectual apprehension, from which her hours of frantic pain seemed far indeed removed. He had done this thing under the same roof with her – his wife. He had not frankly loved the younger woman, broken with his wife, made a new marriage. That would have been heart-break pure and simple. This was something else.

That letter, that wretched, cold, carefully guarded, unsigned letter, that bill – far safer than a cheque – these did not speak of affection. Some men can love two women at one time. This was not love.

Mrs Marroner's sense of pity and outrage for herself, the

wife, now spread suddenly into a perception of pity and outrage for the girl. All that splendid, clean young beauty, the hope of a happy life, with marriage and motherhood, honourable independence, even – these were nothing to that man. For his own pleasure he had chosen to rob her of her life's best joys.

He would 'take care of her', said the letter. How? In what capacity?

And then, sweeping over both her feelings for herself, the wife, and Gerta, his victim, came a new flood, which literally lifted her to her feet. She rose and walked, her head held high. 'This is the sin of man against woman,' she said. 'The offence is against womanhood. Against motherhood. Against – the child.'

She stopped.

The child. His child. That, too, he sacrificed and injured – doomed to degradation.

When Mr Marroner reached home a few weeks later, following his letters too soon to expect an answer to either, he saw no wife upon the pier, though he had cabled, and found the house closed darkly. He let himself in with his latch-key, and stole softly upstairs, to surprise his wife.

No wife was there.

He rang the bell. No servant answered it.

He turned up light after light, searched the house from top to bottom; it was utterly empty. The kitchen wore a clean, bald, unsympathetic aspect. He left it and slowly mounted the stairs, completely dazed. The whole house was clean, in perfect order, wholly vacant.

One thing he felt perfectly sure of – she knew.

Yet was he sure? He must not assume too much. She might have been ill. She might have died. He started to his feet. No, they would have cabled him. He sat down again.

For any such change, if she had wanted him to know, she would have written. Perhaps she had, and he, returning so suddenly, had missed the letter. The thought was some comfort. It must be so. He turned to the telephone and again hesitated. If she had found out – if she had gone – utterly gone, without a word – should he announce it himself to friends and family?

He walked the floor; he searched everywhere for some letter, some word of explanation. Again and again he went to the telephone – and always stopped. He could not bear to ask: 'Do you know where my wife is?'

The harmonious, beautiful rooms reminded him in a dumb, helpless way of her – like the remote smile on the face of the dead. He put out the lights, could not bear the darkness, turned them all on again.

It was a long night –

In the morning he went early to the office. In the accumulated mail was no letter from her. No one seemed to know of anything unusual. A friend asked after his wife – 'Pretty glad to see you, I guess?' He answered evasively.

About eleven a man came to see him: John Hill, her lawyer. Her cousin, too. Mr Marroner had never liked him. He liked him less now, for Mr Hill merely handed him a letter, remarked, 'I was requested to deliver this to you personally,' and departed, looking like a person who is called on to kill something offensive.

'I have gone. I will care for Gerta. Goodbye. Marion.'

That was all. There was no date, no address, no postmark, nothing but that.

In his anxiety and distress, he had fairly forgotten Gerta and all that. Her name aroused in him a sense of rage. She had come between him and his wife. She had taken his wife from him. That was the way he felt.

At first he said nothing, did nothing, lived on alone in his house, taking meals where he chose. When people asked him about his wife, he said she was travelling – for her health. He would not have it in the newspapers. Then, as time passed, as no enlightenment came to him, he resolved not to bear it any longer, and employed detectives. They blamed him for not having put them on the track earlier, but set to work, urged to the utmost secrecy.

What to him had been so blank a wall of mystery seemed not to embarrass them in the least. They made careful inquiries as to her 'past', found where she had studied, where taught, and on what lines; that she had some little money of her own, that her doctor was Josephine L. Bleet, MD, and many other bits of information.

As a result of careful and prolonged work, they finally told him that she had resumed teaching under one of her old professors, lived quietly, and apparently kept boarders; giving him town, street, and number, as if it were a matter of no difficulty whatever.

He had returned in early spring. It was autumn before he found her.

A quiet college town in the hills, a broad, shady street, a pleasant house standing in its own lawn, with trees and flowers about it. He had the address in his hand, and the number showed clear on the white gate. He walked up the straight gravel path and rang the bell. An elderly servant opened the door.

'Does Mrs Marroner live here?'

'No, sir.'

'This is number twenty-eight?'

'Yes, sir.'

'Who does live here?'

'Miss Wheeling, sir.'

Ah! Her maiden name. They had told him, but he had forgotten.

He stepped inside. 'I would like to see her,' he said.

He was ushered into a still parlour, cool and sweet with the scent of flowers, the flowers she had always loved best. It almost brought tears to his eyes. All their years of happiness rose in his mind again – the exquisite beginnings; the days of eager longing before she was really his; the deep, still beauty of her love.

Surely she would forgive him – she must forgive him. He would humble himself; he would tell her of his honest remorse – his absolute determination to be a different man.

Through the wide doorway there came in to him two women. One like a tall Madonna, bearing a baby in her arms.

Marion, calm, steady, definitely impersonal, nothing but a clear pallor to hint of inner stress.

Gerta, holding the child as a bulwark, with a new intelligence in her face, and her blue, adoring eyes fixed on her friend – not upon him.

He looked from one to the other dumbly.

And the woman who had been his wife asked quietly:

'What have you to say to us?'

ETHEL PHELPS JOHNSON

Gawain and the Lady Ragnell

Long ago, in the days of King Arthur, the finest knight in all Britain was the king's nephew Gawain. He was, by reputation, the bravest in battle, the wisest, the most courteous, the most compassionate, and the most loyal to his king.

One day in late summer, Gawain was with Arthur and the knights of the court at Carlisle in the north. The King returned from the day's hunting looking so pale and shaken that Gawain followed him at once to his chamber.

'What has happened, my lord?' asked Gawain with concern.

Arthur sat down heavily. 'I had a very strange encounter in Inglewood forest . . . I hardly know what to make of it.' And he related to Gawain what had occurred.

'Today I hunted a great white stag,' said Arthur. 'The stag at last escaped me and I was alone, some distance from my men. Suddenly a tall, powerful man appeared before me with sword upraised.'

'And you were unarmed!'

'Yes. I had only my bow and a dagger in my belt. He threatened to kill me,' Arthur went on. 'And he swung his sword as though he meant to cut me down on the spot! Then he laughed horribly and said he would give me one chance to save my life.'

'Who was this man?' cried Gawain. 'Why should he want to kill you?'

'He said his name was Sir Gromer, and he sought revenge for the loss of his northern lands.'

'A chieftain from the north!' exclaimed Gawain. 'But what is this one chance he spoke of?'

'I gave him my word I would meet him one year from today, unarmed, at the same spot, with the answer to a question!' said Arthur.

Gawain started to laugh, but stopped at once when he saw Arthur's face. 'A question! Is it a riddle? And one year to find the answer? That should not be hard!'

'If I can bring him the true answer to the question, "What is it that women most desire, above all else?" my life will be spared.' Arthur scowled. 'He is sure I will fail. It must be a foolish riddle that no one can answer.'

'My lord, we have one year to search the kingdom for answers,' said Gawain confidently. 'I will help you. Surely one of the answers will be the right one.'

'No doubt you are right – someone will know the answer.' Arthur looked more cheerful. 'The man is mad, but a chieftain will keep his word.'

For the next twelve months, Arthur and Gawain asked the question from one corner of the kingdom to the other. Then at last the appointed day drew near. Although they had many answers, Arthur was worried.

'With so many answers to choose from, how do we know which is the right one?' he asked in despair. 'Not one of them has the ring of truth.'

A few days before he was to meet Sir Gromer, Arthur rode out alone through the golden gorse and purple heather. The track led upward towards a grove of great oaks. Arthur, deep in thought, did not look up until he reached the edge of the oak wood. When he raised his head, he pulled up suddenly in astonishment.

Before him was a grotesque woman. She was almost as wide as she was high, her skin was mottled green, and spikes of weedlike hair covered her head. Her face seemed more animal than human.

The woman's eyes met Arthur's fearlessly. 'You are Arthur the King,' she said in a harsh, croaking voice. 'In two days' time you must meet Sir Gromer with the answer to a question.'

Arthur turned cold with fear. He stammered, 'Yes . . . yes . . . that is true. Who are you? How did you know of this?'

'I am the Lady Ragnell. Sir Gromer is my stepbrother. You haven't found the true answer, have you?'

'I have many answers,' Arthur replied curtly. 'I do not see how my business concerns you.' He gathered up the reins, eager to be gone.

'You do not have the right answer.' Her certainty filled him with a sense of doom. The harsh voice went on, 'But I know the answer to Sir Gromer's question.'

Arthur turned back in hope and disbelief. 'You do? Tell me the true answer to his question, and I will give you a large bag of gold.'

'I have no use for gold,' she said coldly.

'Nonsense, my good woman. With gold you can buy anything you want!' He hesitated a moment, for the huge, grotesque face with the cool, steady eyes unnerved him. He went on hurriedly, 'What is it you want? Jewellery? Land? Whatever you want I will pay you – that is, if you truly have the right answer.'

'I know the answer. I promise you that!' She paused. 'What I demand in return is that the knight Gawain become my husband.'

There was a moment of shocked silence. Then Arthur cried, 'Impossible! You ask the impossible, woman!'

She shrugged and turned to leave.

'Wait, wait a moment!' Rage and panic overwhelmed him, but he tried to speak reasonably.

'I offer you gold, land, jewels. I cannot give you my nephew. He is his own man. He is not mine to give!'

'I did not ask you to *give* me the knight Gawain,' she rebuked him. 'If Gawain himself agrees to marry me, I will give you the answer. Those are my terms.'

'Impossible!' he sputtered. 'I could not bring him such a proposal.'

'If you should change your mind, I will be here tomorrow,' said she, and disappeared into the oak woods.

Shaken from the weird encounter, Arthur rode homeward at

a slow pace.

'Save my own life at Gawain's expense? Never!' he thought. 'Loathsome woman! I could not even speak of it to Gawain.'

But the afternoon air was soft and sweet with birdsong, and the fateful meeting with Sir Gromer weighed on him heavily. He was torn by the terrible choice facing him.

Gawain rode out from the castle to meet the King. Seeing Arthur's pale, strained face, he exclaimed, 'My lord! Are you ill? What has happened?'

'Nothing . . . nothing at all.' But he could not keep silent long. 'The colossal impudence of the woman! A monster, that's what she is! That creature, daring to give me terms!'

'Calm yourself, uncle,' Gawain said patiently. 'What woman? Terms for what?'

Arthur sighed. 'She knows the answer to the question. I didn't intend to tell you.'

'Why not? Surely that's good news! What is the answer?'

'She will not tell me until her terms are met,' said the King heavily. 'But I assure you, I refuse to consider her proposal!'

Gawain smiled. 'You talk in riddles yourself, uncle. Who is this woman who claims to know the answer? What is her proposal?'

Seeing Gawain's smiling, expectant face, Arthur at first could not speak. Then, with his eyes averted, the King told Gawain the whole story, leaving out no detail.

'The Lady Ragnell is Sir Gromer's stepsister? Yes, I think she would know the right answer,' Gawain said thoughtfully. 'How fortunate that I will be able to save your life!'

'No! I will not let you sacrifice yourself!' Arthur cried.

'It is my choice and my decision,' Gawain answered. 'I will return with you tomorrow and agree to the marriage – on condition that the answer she supplies is the right one to save your life.'

Early the following day, Gawain rode out with Arthur. But not even meeting the loathsome lady face to face could shake his resolve. Her proposal was accepted.

Gawain bowed courteously. 'If on the morrow your answer saves the king's life, we will be wed.'

On the fateful morning, Gawain watched the King stow a

parchment in his saddlebag. 'I'll try all these answers first,' said Arthur.

They rode together for the first part of the journey. Then Arthur, unarmed as agreed, rode on alone to Inglewood to meet Sir Gromer.

The tall, powerful chieftain was waiting, his broadsword glinting in the sun.

Arthur read off one answer, then another, and another. Sir Gromer shook his head in satisfaction.

'No, you have not the right answer!' he said raising his sword high. 'You've failed, and now –'

'Wait!' Arthur cried. 'I have one more answer. What a woman desires above all else is the power of sovereignty – the right to exercise her own will.'

With a loud oath the man dropped his sword. 'You did not find that answer by yourself!' he shouted. 'My cursed stepsister, Ragnell, gave it to you. Bold, interfering hussy! I'll run her through with my sword . . . I'll lop off her head . . .' Turning, he plunged into the forest, a string of horrible curses echoing behind him.

Arthur rode back to where Gawain waited with the monstrous Ragnell. They returned to the castle in silence. Only the grotesque Lady Ragnell seemed in good spirits.

The news spread quickly throughout the castle. Gawain, the finest knight in the land, was to marry this monstrous creature! Some tittered and laughed at the spectacle; others said the Lady Ragnell must possess very great lands and estates; but mostly there was stunned silence.

Arthur took his nephew aside nervously. 'Must you go through with it at once? A postponement perhaps?'

Gawain looked at him steadily. 'I gave my promise, my lord. The Lady Ragnell's answer saved your life. Would you have me –'

'Your loyalty makes me ashamed! Of course you cannot break your word.' And Arthur turned away.

The marriage took place in the abbey. Afterwards, with Gawain and the Lady Ragnell sitting at the high dais table beside the King and Queen, the strange wedding feast began.

'She takes the space of two women on the chair,' muttered the knight Gareth. 'Poor Gawain!'

'I would not marry such a creature for all the land in Christendom!' answered his companion.

An uneasy silence settled on the hall. Only the monstrous Lady Ragnell displayed good spirits and good appetite. Throughout the long day and evening, Gawain remained pleasant and courteous. In no way did his manner towards his strange bride show other than kind attention.

The wedding feast drew to a close. Gawain and his bride were conducted to their chamber and were at last alone.

The Lady Ragnell gazed at her husband thoughtfully.

'You have kept your promise well and faithfully,' she observed.

Gawain inclined his head. 'I could not do less, my lady.'

'You've shown neither revulsion nor pity,' she said. After a pause she went on, 'Come now, we are wedded! I am waiting to be kissed.'

Gawain went to her at once and kissed her. When he stepped back, there stood before him a slender young woman with grey eyes and a serene, smiling face.

His scalp tingled in shock. 'What manner of sorcery is this?' he cried hoarsely.

'Do you prefer me in this form?' she smiled and turned slowly in a full circle.

But Gawain backed away warily. 'I . . . yes . . . of course . . . but I don't understand . . .' For this sudden evidence of sorcery, with its unknown powers, made him confused and uneasy.

'My stepbrother, Sir Gromer, had always hated me,' said the Lady Ragnell. 'Unfortunately, through his mother, he has a knowledge of sorcery, and so he changed me into a monstrous creature. He said I must live in that shape until I could persuade the greatest knight in Britain to willingly choose me for his bride. He said it would be an impossible condition to meet!'

'Why did he hate you so cruelly?'

Her lips curled in amusement. 'He thought me bold and unwomanly because I defied him. I refused his commands both for my property and my person.'

Gawain said with admiration, 'You won the "impossible" condition he set, and now his evil spell is broken!'

'Only in part.' Her clear grey eyes held his. 'You have a

choice, my dear Gawain, which way I will be. Would you have me in this, my own shape, at night and my former ugly shape by day? Or would you have me grotesque at night in our chamber, and my own shape in the castle by day? Think carefully before you choose.'

Gawain was silent only a moment. He knelt before her and touched her hand.

'It is a choice I cannot make, my dear Ragnell. It concerns you. Whatever you choose to be – fair by day or fair by night – I will willingly abide by it.'

Ragnell released a long, deep breath. The radiance in her face overwhelmed him.

'You have answered well, dearest Gawain, for your answer has broken Gromer's evil spell completely. The last condition he set has been met! For he said that if, after marriage to the greatest knight in Britain, my husband freely gave me the power of choice, the power to exercise my own free will, the wicked enchantment would be broken forever.'

Thus, in wonder and in joy, began the marriage of Gawain and the Lady Ragnell.

CHARLOTTE PERKINS GILMAN

The Yellow Wallpaper

It is very seldom that mere ordinary people like John and myself secure ancestral halls for the summer.

A colonial mansion, a hereditary estate. I would say a haunted house, and reach the height of romantic felicity – but that would be asking too much of fate!

Still I will proudly declare that there is something queer about it.

Else, why should it be let so cheaply? And why have stood so long untenanted?

John laughs at me, of course, but one expects that in marriage.

John is practical in the extreme. He has no patience with faith, an intense horror of superstition, and he scoffs openly at any talk of things not to be felt and seen and put down in figures.

John is a physician, and *perhaps* (I would not say it to a living soul, of course, but this is dead paper and a great relief to my mind) *perhaps* that is one reason I do not get well faster.

You see he does not believe I am sick!

And what can one do?

If a physician of high standing, and one's own husband, assures friends and relatives that there is really nothing the matter with one but temporary nervous depression – a slight hysterical tendency – what is one to do?

My brother is also a physician, and also of high standing, and he says the same thing.

So I take phosphates or phosphites – whichever it is, and tonics, and journeys, and air, and exercise, and am absolutely forbidden to 'work' until I am well again.

Personally, I disagree with their ideas.

Personally, I believe that congenial work, with excitement and change, would do me good.

But what is one to do?

I did write for a while in spite of them; but it *does* exhaust me a good deal – having to be so sly about it, or else meet with heavy opposition.

I sometimes fancy that in my condition if I had less opposition and more society and stimulus – but John says the very worst thing I can do is to think about my condition, and I confess it always makes me feel bad.

So I will let it alone and talk about the house.

The most beautiful place! It is quite alone, standing well back from the road, quite three miles from the village. It makes me think of English places that you read about, for there are hedges and walls and gates that lock, and lots of separate little houses for the gardeners and people.

There is a *delicious* garden! I never saw such a garden – large and shady, full of box-bordered paths, and lined with long grape-covered arbours with seats under them.

There were greenhouses, too, but they are all broken now.

There was some legal trouble, I believe, something about the heirs and co-heirs; anyhow, the place has been empty for years.

That spoils my ghostliness, I am afraid, but I don't care – there is something strange about the house – I can feel it.

I even said so to John one moonlight evening, but he said what I felt was a *draught*, and shut the window.

I get unreasonably angry with John sometimes. I'm sure I never used to be so sensitive. I think it is due to this nervous condition.

But John says if I feel so, I shall neglect proper self-control; so I take pains to control myself – before him, at least, and that makes me very tired.

I don't like our room a bit. I wanted one downstairs that opened on the piazza and had roses all over the window, and such pretty old-fashioned chintz hangings! But John would not hear of it.

He said there was only one window and not room for two beds, and no near room for him if he took another.

He is very careful and loving, and hardly lets me stir without special direction.

I have a schedule prescription for each hour in the day; he takes all care from me, and so I feel basely ungrateful not to value it more.

He said we came here solely on my account, that I was to have perfect rest and all the air I could get. 'Your exercise depends on your strength, my dear,' said he, 'and your food somewhat on your appetite; but air you can absorb all the time.' So we took the nursery at the top of the house.

It is a big, airy room, the whole floor nearly, with windows that look all ways, and air and sunshine galore. It was nursery first and then playroom and gymnasium, I should judge; for the windows are barred for little children, and there are rings and things in the walls.

The paint and paper look as if a boys' school had used it. It is stripped off – the paper – in great patches all around the head of my bed, about as far as I can reach, and in a great place on the other side of the room low down. I never saw a worse paper in my life.

One of those sprawling flamboyant patterns committing every artistic sin.

It is dull enough to confuse the eye in following, pronounced enough to constantly irritate and provoke study, and when you follow the lame uncertain curves for a little distance they suddenly commit suicide – plunge off at outrageous angles, destroy themselves in unheard of contradictions.

The colour is repellent, almost revolting; a smouldering unclean yellow, strangely faded by the slow-turning sunlight.

It is a dull yet lurid orange in some places, a sickly sulphur tint in others.

No wonder the children hated it! I should hate it myself if I had to live in this room long.

There comes John, and I must put this away, – he hates to have me write a word.

* * *

We have been here two weeks, and I haven't felt like writing before, since that first day.

I am sitting by the window now, up in this atrocious nursery, and there is nothing to hinder my writing as much as I please, save lack of strength.

John is away all day, and even some nights when his cases are serious.

I am glad my case is not serious!

But these nervous troubles are dreadfully depressing.

John does not know how much I really suffer. He knows there is no *reason* to suffer, and that satisfies him.

Of course it is only nervousness. It does weigh on me so not to do my duty in any way!

I meant to be such a help to John, such a real rest and comfort, and here I am a comparative burden already!

Nobody would believe what an effort it is to do what little I am able – to dress and entertain, and order things.

It is fortunate Mary is so good with the baby. Such a dear baby!

And yet I *cannot* be with him, it makes me so nervous.

I suppose John never was nervous in his life. He laughs at me so about this wallpaper!

At first he meant to repaper the room, but afterwards he said that I was letting it get the better of me, and that nothing was worse for a nervous patient than to give way to such fancies.

He said that after the wallpaper was changed it would be the heavy bedstead, and then the barred windows, and then that gate at the head of the stairs, and so on.

'You know the place is doing you good,' he said, 'and really, dear, I don't care to renovate the house just for a three months' rental.'

'Then do let us go downstairs,' I said, 'there are such pretty rooms there.'

Then he took me in his arms and called me a blessed little

goose, and said he would go down into the cellar, if I wished, and have it whitewashed into the bargain.

But he is right enough about the beds and windows and things.

It is as airy and comfortable a room as any one need wish, and, of course, I would not be so silly as to make him uncomfortable just for a whim.

I'm really getting quite fond of the big room, all but that horrid paper.

Out of one window I can see the garden, those mysterious deep-shaded arbours, the riotous old-fashioned flowers, and bushes and gnarly trees.

Out of another I get a lovely view of the bay and a little private wharf belonging to the estate. There is a beautiful shaded lane that runs down there from the house. I always fancy I see people walking in these numerous paths and arbours, but John has cautioned me not to give way to fancy in the least. He says that with my imaginative power and habit of story-making, a nervous weakness like mine is sure to lead to all manner of excited fancies, and that I ought to use my will and good sense to check the tendency. So I try.

I think sometimes that if I were only well enough to write a little it would relieve the press of ideas and rest me.

But I find I get pretty tired when I try.

It is so discouraging not to have any advice and companionship about my work. When I get really well, John says we will ask Cousin Henry and Julia down for a long visit; but he says he would as soon put fireworks in my pillow-case as to let me have those stimulating people about now.

I wish I could get well faster.

But I must not think about that. This paper looks to me as if it *knew* what a vicious influence it had!

There is a recurrent spot where the pattern lolls like a broken neck and two bulbous eyes stare at you upside down.

I get positively angry with the impertinence of it and the everlastingness. Up and down and sideways they crawl, and those absurd, unblinking eyes are everywhere. There is one place where two breadths didn't match, and the eyes go all up and down the line, one a little higher than the other.

I never saw so much expression in an inanimate thing before, and we all know how much expression they have! I used to lie awake as a child and get more entertainment and terror out of blank walls and plain furniture than most children could find in a toy-store.

I remember what a kindly wink the knobs of our big, old bureau used to have, and there was one chair that always seemed like a strong friend.

I used to feel that if any of the other things looked too fierce I could always hop into that chair and be safe.

The furniture in this room is no worse than inharmonious, however, for we had to bring it all from downstairs. I suppose when this was used as a playroom they had to take the nursery things out, and no wonder! I never saw such ravages as the children have made here.

The wallpaper, as I said before, is torn off in spots, and it sticketh closer than a brother – they must have had perseverance as well as hatred.

Then the floor is scratched and gouged and splintered, the plaster itself is dug out here and there, and this great heavy bed which is all we found in the room, looks as if it had been through the wars.

But I don't mind it a bit – only the paper.

There comes John's sister. Such a dear girl as she is, and so careful of me! I must not let her find me writing.

She is a perfect and enthusiastic housekeeper, and hopes for no better profession. I verily believe she thinks it is the writing which made me sick!

But I can write when she is out, and see her a long way off from these windows.

There is one that commands the road, a lovely shaded winding road, and one that just looks off over the country. A lovely country, too, full of great elms and velvet meadows.

This wallpaper has a kind of sub-pattern in a different shade, a particularly irritating one, for you can only see it in certain lights, and not clearly then.

But in the places where it isn't faded and where the sun is just so – I can see a strange, provoking, formless sort of figure, that seems to skulk about behind that silly and conspicuous front design.

There's sister on the stairs!

* * *

Well, the Fourth of July is over! The people are all gone and I am tired out. John thought it might do me good to see a little company, so we just had mother and Nellie and the children down for a week.

Of course I didn't do a thing. Jennie sees to everything now.

But it tired me all the same.

John says if I don't pick up faster he shall send me to Weir Mitchell in the fall.

But I don't want to go there at all. I had a friend who was in his hands once, and she says he is just like John and my brother, only more so!

Besides, it is such an undertaking to go so far.

I don't feel as if it was worth while to turn my hand over for anything, and I'm getting dreadfully fretful and querulous.

I cry at nothing, and cry most of the time.

Of course I don't when John is here, or anybody else, but when I am alone.

And I am alone a good deal just now. John is kept in town very often by serious cases, and Jennie is good and lets me alone when I want her to.

So I walk a little in the garden or down that lovely lane, sit on the porch under the roses, and lie down up here a good deal.

I'm getting really fond of the room in spite of the wallpaper. Perhaps *because* of the wallpaper.

It dwells in my mind so!

I lie here on this great immovable bed – it is nailed down, I believe – and follow that pattern about by the hour. It is as good as gymnastics, I assure you. I start, we'll say, at the bottom, down in the corner over there where it has not been touched, and I determine for the thousandth time that I *will* follow that pointless pattern to some sort of a conclusion.

I know a little of the principle of design, and I know this thing was not arranged on any laws of radiation, or alternation, or repetition, or symmetry, or anything else that I ever heard of.

It is repeated, of course, by the breadths, but not otherwise.

Looked at in one way each breadth stands alone, the bloated curves and flourishes – a kind of 'debased Romanesque' with *delirium tremens* – go waddling up and down in isolated columns of fatuity.

But, on the other hand, they connect diagonally, and the sprawling outlines run off in great slanting waves of optic horror, like a lot of wallowing seaweeds in full chase.

The whole thing goes horizontally, too, at least it seems so, and I exhaust myself in trying to distinguish the order of its going in that direction.

They have used a horizontal breadth for a frieze, and that adds wonderfully to the confusion.

There is one end of the room where it is almost intact, and there, when the crosslights fade and the low sun shines directly upon it, I can almost fancy radiation after all, the interminable grotesques seem to form around a common centre and rush off in headlong plunges of equal distraction.

It makes me tired to follow it. I will take a nap I guess.

* * *

I don't know why I should write this.

I don't want to.

I don't feel able.

And I know John would think it absurd. But I *must* say what I feel and think in some way – it is such a relief!

But the effort is getting to be greater than the relief.

Half the time now I am awfully lazy, and lie down ever so much.

John says I mustn't lose my strength, and has me take cod liver oil and lots of tonics and things, to say nothing of ale and wine and rare meat.

Dear John! He loves me very dearly, and hates to have me sick. I tried to have a real earnest reasonable talk with him the other day, and tell him how I wish he would let me go and make a visit to Cousin Henry and Julia.

But he said I wasn't able to go, nor able to stand it after I got there; and I did not make out a very good case for myself, for I was crying before I had finished.

It is getting to be a great effort for me to think straight. Just this nervous weakness I suppose.

And dear John gathered me up in his arms, and just carried me upstairs and laid me on the bed, and sat by me and read to me till it tired my head.

He said I was his darling and his comfort and all he had, and that I must take care of myself for his sake, and keep well.

He says no one but myself can help me out of it, that I must use my will and self-control and not let any silly fancies run away with me.

There's one comfort, the baby is well and happy, and does not have to occupy this nursery with the horrid wallpaper.

If we had not used it, that blessed child would have! What a fortunate escape! Why, I wouldn't have a child of mine, an impressionable little thing, live in such a room for worlds.

I never thought of it before, but it is lucky that John kept me here after all, I can stand it so much easier than a baby, you see.

Of course I never mention it to them any more – I am too wise – but I keep watch of it all the same.

There are things in that paper that nobody knows but me, or ever will.

Behind that outside pattern the dim shapes get clearer every day.

It is always the same shape, only very numerous.

And it is like a woman stooping down and creeping about behind that pattern. I don't like it a bit. I wonder – I begin to think – I wish John would take me away from here!

* * *

It is so hard to talk with John about my case, because he is so wise, and because he loves me so.

But I tried it last night.

It was moonlight. The moon shines in all around just as the sun does.

I hate to see it sometimes, it creeps so slowly, and always comes in by one window or another.

John was asleep and I hated to waken him, so I kept still and watched the moonlight on that undulating wallpaper till I felt creepy.

The faint figure behind seemed to shake the pattern, just as if she wanted to get out.

I got up softly and went to feel and see if the paper *did* move, and when I came back John was awake.

'What is it, little girl?' he said. 'Don't go walking about like that – you'll get cold.'

I thought it was a good time to talk, so I told him that I really was not gaining here, and that I wished he would take me away.

'Why, darling!' said he, 'our lease will be up in three weeks, and I can't see how to leave before.'

'The repairs are not done at home, and I cannot possibly leave town just now. Of course if you were in any danger, I could and would, but you really are better, dear, whether you can see it or not. I am a doctor, dear, and I know. You are gaining flesh and colour, your appetite is better, I feel really much easier about you.'

'I don't weigh a bit more,' said I, 'nor as much; and my appetite may be better in the evening when you are here, but it is worse in the morning when you are away!'

'Bless her little heart!' said he with a big hug, 'she shall be as sick as she pleases! But now let's improve the shining hours by going to sleep, and talk about it in the morning!'

'And you won't go away?'

'Why, how can I, dear? It is only three weeks more and then we will take a nice little trip of a few days while Jennie is getting the house ready. Really dear you are better!'

'Better in body perhaps –' I began, and stopped short, for he sat up straight and looked at me with such a stern, reproachful look that I could not say another word.

'My darling,' said he, 'I beg of you, for my sake and for our child's sake, as well as for your own, that you will never for one instant let that idea enter your mind! There is nothing so dangerous, so fascinating, to a temperament like yours. It is a false and foolish fancy. Can you not trust me as a physician when I tell you so?'

So of course I said no more on that score, and we went to sleep before long. He thought I was asleep first, but I wasn't, and lay there for hours trying to decide whether that front pattern and the back pattern really did move together or separately.

* * *

On a pattern like this, by daylight, there is a lack of sequence, a defiance of law, that is a constant irritant to a normal mind.

The colour is hideous enough, and unreliable enough, and infuriating enough, but the pattern is torturing.

You think you have mastered it, but just as you get well underway in following, it turns a back-somersault and there you are. It slaps you in the face, knocks you down, and tramples upon you. It is like a bad dream.

The outside pattern is a florid arabesque, reminding one of a fungus. If you can imagine a toadstool in joints, an interminable string of toadstools, budding and sprouting in endless convolutions – why, that is something like it.

That is, sometimes!

There is one marked peculiarity about this paper, a thing nobody seems to notice but myself, and that is that it changes as the light changes.

When the sun shoots in through the east window – I always watch for that first long, straight ray – it changes so quickly that I never can quite believe it.

That is why I watch it always.

By moonlight – the moon shines in all night when there is a moon – I wouldn't know it was the same paper.

At night in any kind of light, in twilight, candlelight, lamplight, and worst of all by moonlight, it becomes bars! The outside pattern I mean, and the woman behind it is as plain as can be.

I didn't realise for a long time what the thing was that showed behind, that dim sub-pattern, but now I am quite sure it is a woman.

By daylight she is subdued, quiet. I fancy it is the pattern that keeps her so still. It is so puzzling. It keeps me quiet by the hour.

I lie down ever so much now. John says it is good for me, and to sleep all I can.

Indeed he started the habit by making me lie down for an hour after each meal.

It is a very bad habit I am convinced, for you see I don't sleep.

And that cultivates deceit, for I don't tell them I'm awake – O no!

The fact is I am getting a little afraid of John.

He seems very queer sometimes, and even Jennie has an

inexplicable look.

It strikes me occasionally, just as a scientific hypothesis – that perhaps it is the paper!

I have watched John when he did not know I was looking, and come into the room suddenly on the most innocent excuses, and I've caught him several times *looking at the paper*! And Jennie too. I caught Jennie with her hand on it once.

She didn't know I was in the room, and when I asked her in a quiet, a very quiet voice, with the most restrained manner possible, what she was doing with the paper – she turned around as if she had been caught stealing, and looked quite angry – asked me why I should frighten her so!

Then she said that the paper stained everything it touched, that she had found yellow smooches on all my clothes and John's, and she wished we would be more careful!

Did not that sound innocent? But I know she was studying that pattern, and I am determined that nobody shall find it out but myself!

* * *

Life is very much more exciting now than it used to be. You see I have something more to expect, to look forward to, to watch. I really do eat better, and am more quiet than I was.

John is so pleased to see me improve! He laughed a little the other day, and said I seemed to be flourishing in spite of my wallpaper.

I turned it off with a laugh. I had no intention of telling him it was *because* of the wallpaper – he would make fun of me. He might even want to take me away.

I don't want to leave now until I have found it out. There is a week more, and I think that will be enough.

* * *

I'm feeling ever so much better! I don't sleep much at night, for it is so interesting to watch developments; but I sleep a good deal in the daytime.

In the daytime it is tiresome and perplexing.

There are always new shoots on the fungus, and new shades of yellow all over it. I cannot keep count of them, though I have tried conscientiously.

It is the strangest yellow, that wallpaper! It makes me think of all the yellow things I ever saw – not beautiful ones like buttercups, but old foul, bad yellow things.

But there is something else about that paper – the smell! I noticed it the moment we came into the room, but with so much air and sun it was not bad. Now we have had a week of fog and rain, and whether the windows are open or not, the smell is here.

It creeps all over the house.

I find it hovering in the dining-room, skulking in the parlour, hiding in the hall, lying in wait for me on the stairs.

It gets into my hair.

Even when I go to ride, if I turn my head suddenly and surprise it – there is that smell!

Such a peculiar odour, too! I have spent hours in trying to analyse it, to find what it smelled like.

It is not bad – at first, and very gentle, but quite the subtlest, most enduring odour I ever met.

In this damp weather it is awful. I wake up in the night and find it hanging over me.

It used to disturb me at first. I thought seriously of burning the house – to reach the smell.

But now I am used to it. The only thing I can think of that it is like is the *colour* of the paper! A yellow smell.

There is a very funny mark on this wall, low down, near the mopboard. A streak that runs round the room. It goes behind every piece of furniture, except the bed, a long, straight, even *smooch*, as if it had been rubbed over and over.

I wonder how it was done and who did it, and what they did it for. Round and round and round – round and round and round! – it makes me dizzy!

* * *

I really have discovered something at last.

Through watching so much at night, when it changes so, I have finally found out.

The front pattern *does* move – and no wonder! The woman behind shakes it!

Sometimes I think there are a great many women behind, and

sometimes only one, and she crawls around fast, and her crawling shakes it all over.

Then in the very bright spots she keeps still, and in the very shady spots she just takes hold of the bars and shakes them hard.

And she is all the time trying to climb through. But nobody could climb through that pattern – it strangles so; I think that is why it has so many heads.

They get through, and then the pattern strangles them off and turns them upside down, and makes their eyes white!

If those heads were covered or taken off it would not be half so bad.

* * *

I think that woman gets out in the daytime!

And I'll tell you why – privately – I've seen her!

It is the same woman, I know, for she is always creeping, and most women do not creep by daylight.

I see her in that long shaded lane, creeping up and down. I see her in those dark grape arbours, creeping all around the garden.

I see her on that long road under the trees, creeping along, and when a carriage comes she hides under the blackberry vines.

I don't blame her a bit. It must be very humiliating to be caught creeping by daylight!

I always lock the door when I creep by daylight. I can't do it at night, for I know John would suspect something at once.

And John is so queer now, that I don't want to irritate him. I wish he would take another room! Besides, I don't want anybody to get that woman out at night but myself.

I often wonder if I could see her out of all the windows at once.

But, turn as fast as I can, I can only see out of one at one time.

And though I always see her, she *may* be able to creep faster than I can turn!

I have watched her sometimes away off in the open country, creeping as fast as a cloud shadow in a high wind.

* * *

If only that top pattern could be gotten off from the under one! I mean to try it, little by little.

I have found out another funny thing, but I shan't tell it this time! It does not do to trust people too much.

There are only two more days to get this paper off, and I believe John is beginning to notice. I don't like the look in his eyes.

And I heard him ask Jennie a lot of professional questions about me. She had a very good report to give.

She said I slept a good deal in the daytime.

John knows I don't sleep very well at night, for all I'm so quiet!

He asked me all sorts of questions, too, and pretended to be very loving and kind.

As if I couldn't see through him!

Still, I don't wonder he acts so, sleeping under this paper for three months.

It only interests me, but I feel sure John and Jennie are secretly affected by it.

* * *

Hurrah! This is the last day, but it is enough. John is to stay in town over night, and won't be out until this evening.

Jennie wanted to sleep with me – the sly thing! But I told her I should undoubtedly rest better for a night all alone.

That was clever, for really I wasn't alone a bit! As soon as it was moonlight and that poor thing began to crawl and shake the pattern, I got up and ran to help her.

I pulled and she shook, I shook and she pulled, and before morning we had peeled off yards of that paper.

A strip about as high as my head and half around the room.

And then when the sun came and that awful pattern began to laugh at me, I declared I would finish it today!

We go away tomorrow, and they are moving all my furniture down again to leave things as they were before.

Jennie looked at the wall in amazement, but I told her merrily that I did it out of pure spite at the vicious thing.

She laughed and said she wouldn't mind doing it herself, but I must not get tired.

How she betrayed herself that time!

But I am here, and no person touches this paper but me – not *alive*!

She tried to get me out of the room – it was too patent! But I said it was so quiet and empty and clean now that I believed I would lie down again and sleep all I could; and not to wake me even for dinner – I would call when I woke.

So now she is gone, and the servants are gone, and the things are gone, and there is nothing left but that great bedstead nailed down, with the canvas mattress we found on it.

We shall sleep downstairs tonight, and take the boat home tomorrow.

I quite enjoy the room, now it is bare again.

How those children did tear about here!

This bedstead is fairly gnawed.

But I must get to work.

I have locked the door and thrown the key down into the front path.

I don't want to go out, and I don't want to have anybody come in, till John comes.

I want to astonish him.

I've got a rope up here that even Jennie did not find. If that woman does get out, and tries to get away, I can tie her!

But I forgot I could not reach far without anything to stand on!

This bed will *not* move!

I tried to lift and push it until I was lame, and then I got so angry I bit off a little piece at one corner – but it hurt my teeth.

Then I peeled off all the paper I could reach standing on the floor. It sticks horribly and the pattern just enjoys it! All those strangled heads and bulbous eyes and waddling fungus growths just shriek with derision!

I am getting angry enough to do something desperate. To jump out of the window would be admirable exercise, but the bars are too strong even to try.

Besides I wouldn't do it. Of course not. I know well enough that a step like that is improper and might be misconstrued.

I don't like to *look* out of the windows even – there are so many of those creeping women, and they creep so fast.

I wonder if they all come out of that wallpaper as I did?

But I am securely fastened now by my well-hidden rope – you don't get *me* out in the road there!

I suppose I shall have to get back behind the pattern when it comes night, and that is hard!

It is so pleasant to be out in this great room and creep around as I please!

I don't want to go outside. I won't, even if Jennie asks me to.

For outside you have to creep on the ground, and everything is green instead of yellow.

But here I can creep smoothly on the floor, and my shoulder just fits in that long smooch around the wall, so I cannot lose my way.

Why there's John at the door!

It is no use, young man, you can't open it!

How he does call and pound!

Now he's crying for an axe.

It would be a shame to break down that beautiful door!

'John dear!' said I in the gentlest voice, 'the key is down by the front steps, under a plantain leaf!'

That silenced him for a few moments.

Then he said – very quietly indeed, 'Open the door, my darling!'

'I can't,' said I. 'The key is down by the front door under a plantain leaf!'

And then I said it again, several times, very gently and slowly, and said it so often that he had to go and see, and he got it of course, and came in. He stopped short by the door.

'What is the matter?' he cried. 'For God's sake, what are you doing!'

I kept on creeping just the same, but I looked at him over my shoulder.

'I've got out at last,' said I, 'in spite of you and Jennie. And I've pulled off most of the paper, so you can't put me back!'

Now why should that man have fainted? But he did, and right across my path by the wall, so that I had to creep over him every time!

Why I Wrote 'The Yellow Wallpaper'
by Charlotte Perkins Gilman

Many and many a reader has asked that. When the story first came out, in the *New England Magazine* about 1891, a Boston physician made protest in *The Transcript*. Such a story ought not to be written, he said; it was enough to drive anyone mad to read it.

Another physician, in Kansas I think, wrote to say that it was the best description of incipient insanity he had ever seen, and – begging my pardon – had I been there?

Now the story of the story is this:

For many years I suffered from a severe and continuous nervous breakdown tending to melancholia – and beyond. During about the third year of this trouble I went, in devout faith and some faint stir of hope, to a noted specialist in nervous diseases, the best known in the country. This wise man put me to bed and applied the rest cure, to which a still-good physique responded so promptly that he concluded there was nothing much the matter with me, and sent me home with solemn advice to 'live as domestic a life as far as possible,' to 'have but two hours' intellectual life a day', and 'never to touch pen, brush, or pencil again' as long as I lived. This was in 1887.

I went home and obeyed those directions for some three months, and came so near the borderline of utter mental ruin that I could see over.

Then, using the remnants of intelligence that remained, and helped by a wise friend, I cast the noted specialist's advice to the winds and went to work again – work, the normal life of every human being; work, in which is joy and growth and service, without which one is a pauper and a parasite – ultimately recovering some measure of power.

Being naturally moved to rejoicing by this narrow escape, I wrote 'The Yellow Wallpaper', with its embellishments and additions, to carry out the ideal (I never had hallucinations or objections to my mural decorations) and sent a copy to the physician who so nearly drove me mad. He never acknowledged it.

The little book is valued by alienists and as a good specimen of one kind of literature. It has, to my knowledge, saved one woman from a similar fate – so terrifying her family that they let her out into normal activity and she recovered.

But the best result is this. Many years later I was told that the great specialist had admitted to friends of his that he had altered his treatment of neurasthenia since reading 'The Yellow Wallpaper'.

It was not intended to drive people crazy, but to save people from being driven crazy, and it worked.

Follow On

The aim of all the activities in this section is to add to your enjoyment and understanding of the stories in this anthology. Some stories you may simply want to read and remember, others you may want to talk and write about, others may spark off memories and further ideas.

The suggestions for activities can be used to help you build up a folder for the coursework element of the General Certificate of Secondary Education. These activities fall into three broad areas:

Before reading – enabling you to anticipate and speculate about what is going to happen.

During reading – building up a picture of what is going on and what may happen next.

After reading – allowing time to reflect on the setting, events, characters, issues and themes within the stories; giving opportunities for discussion, and for personal, critical and discursive writing.

Many of the activities will involve a mixture of individual, group and whole class work. You may not want to attempt all of the suggested activities but choose ones which particularly interest you. In some cases you may prefer to devise an activity of your own.

General Activities

Before reading

▶ Read an extract, poem, play or short story which:
  – takes up similar themes or issues
  – presents characters/settings in similar/contrasting ways
  – is written in a similar/contrasting style or genre.

▶ Take some general issues or questions raised in the story and discuss them in advance to find out how much you and others know and what opinions you have about them. After reading the story, discuss how far your ideas and opinions may have changed.

▶ Use the titles and/or the first few paragraphs to speculate and predict what the story may be about.

▶ Take some quotations from the story and speculate how the story will develop.

| During reading |

▶ Stop at various points during reading, and review what has happened so far, then predict what might happen next or how the story may develop.

▶ Stop at various points and discuss why writers have made certain decisions and what alternatives were open to them.

▶ Decide who is telling or speaking the story.

▶ Look out for quotations that help reveal the meaning of the story.

▶ Make notes and observations on plot, character, relationships between characters, style and the way the narrative works.

▶ Consider the various issues, themes or questions relating to the story which you discussed before reading.

▶ Build up a visual picture of the setting in order to work out its significance in the story or to represent it as a diagram.

| After reading |

▶ Discuss a number of statements about the story and decide which best conveys what the story is about.

▶ Prepare a dramatic reading of parts of the text.

▶ Use the story as a stimulus for personal and imaginative writing:
  – writing stories/plays/poems on a similar theme
  – writing stories/plays/poems in a similar style, genre or with a similar structure.

▶ Discuss and write imaginative reconstructions or extensions of the text:
  – rewriting the story from another character's point of view
  – writing a scene which occurs before the story begins
  – continuing beyond the end of the story
  – writing an alternative ending
  – changing the narrative from first to the third person and vice versa
  – experimenting with style and form

- picking a point in the story where the action takes a turn in direction and rewriting the rest of the story in a different way.

▶ Represent some of the ideas, issues and themes in the story for a particular purpose and audience:
  - enacting a public inquiry or tribunal
  - conducting an interview for TV or radio
  - writing a newspaper report or press release
  - writing a letter to a specified person or organisation
  - giving an eye-witness report.

▶ Select passages from the story for film or radio scripting; act out the rehearsed script for a live audience, audio or video taping.

▶ Write critically or discursively about the story, or comparing one or more story, focusing on:
  - the meaning of the title
  - character, plot and structure
  - style, tone, use of dialect, language
  - build up of tension, use of climax, humour, pathos, etc.
  - settings
  - endings
  - themes and issues.

Raymond's Run

Before reading

▶ In pairs or small groups spend some time talking about:
  - the things you enjoyed doing when you were seven or eight
  - the things you were expected to do at that age
  - the things you hated doing.

   Make a list or diagram of these points as if you were planning a piece of autobiographical writing about yourself at this age.

During reading

▶ This story is written in a 'tell-it-like-it-is', conversational style as if the narrator is speaking directly to the reader, not as an adult reflecting on childhood but as the child herself living through it. Look for examples of this style while you are reading and for other aspects of the language which strike you.

▶ Half-way through the story the narrator observes that 'girls never really smile at each other because they don't know how and don't want to know how and there's probably no one to teach us how, cause grown-up girls don't know either' (page 10). Look out for the reasons she has for making this statement and the reasons she has for maybe changing her mind.

▶ Make a note of features in the story which identify where it is set.

▶ Write a description of Hazel (her looks, personality, likes, dislikes, the way she sees the world) from what she tells you about herself in the story.

▶ Write short descriptions of Hazel as she is seen by three or four other characters in the story. Write in the style they would use if they were talking to you about her. Finish your writing by saying what you think of her, also using a conversational style.

▶ Use the last sentence of the story as a title and write about what it suggests to you. For example:
   – Are girls encouraged to be something they're not or is it fun being these things as well? Is it the same for boys?
   – Are genuine friendships between girls difficult to come by? Is it the same for boys? Does this change as you get older?
   – In the story, what is it that makes Hazel change her mind about girls' friendships?

▶ 'Grown-ups got a lot of nerve sometimes' (page 12). Use this as a title for *either* a story *or* an essay about the differences of opinion which sometimes exist between adults and children. Try to make your writing humorous, if possible!

▶ Write a report of the 'May Day Races' for the local newspaper in which you capture a balance between the event as a whole and some of the individuals who took part. Or you could do this as a series of taped interviews, improvising in groups.

Flame on the Frontier

▶ What might be the setting or subject matter of this story, judging by the title? In what contexts have you come across the word 'frontier'?

▶ People from different cultures can have varying traditions:
  – they may like different foods and prepare and eat them differently
  – they may choose their names differently
  – they will have special festivals and occasions which they celebrate and honour
  – they may have different religious beliefs
  – they may even have different ideas about what is good or bad behaviour, what is specially praised and what is frowned on in a person.
  Within each of these areas there may also be some similarities.
  In groups, talk about your knowledge of different cultures, covering some of the topics mentioned above.

During reading

▶ Look out for the similarities and differences in culture between the Sioux Indians and frontier settlers in the story, especially in the following areas:
  – their expectations of the way young girls and boys should behave
  – their attitudes to women's work and men's work
  – their rituals of courtship and marriage
  – what is considered to be good and bad behaviour
  – examples of the way both types of settlement are socially organised.

▶ 'Flame on the Frontier' is written in a very direct style; events are sharply reported. Also the narrative jumps about in time, letting the reader know about future events before they occur. While you are reading look out for examples of both these aspects of story-telling.

▶ Stop reading after the words 'They knew what had to be done; they had planned it, because this day might come to any frontier farm' (page 17). In pairs, spend some time predicting what the family's plan might be.

▶ Some words may be unfamiliar to you. Here is a short glossary:
  counted coup – hit an enemy
  travois – platform or net dragged along the ground
  pemmican – preparation of dried, pounded buffalo meat and melted fat
  skillet – cooking pot

After reading

▶ In pairs, re-read the story carefully and using a chart similar to the one below note down the major events or points in the lives of Hannah, Mary Amanda and Sarah Harris mentioned in the story.

Dates	Hannah	Mary Amanda	Sarah
Sun. pm	(Family attacked. Father and 2 brothers killed.)		
Aug. 1862	Gave baby to Johnny – ('dull boy'). 'You take care of him and don't let him go until they kill you' (page 18). Made a brave decoy attempt. Captured. Escaped. Joined another settlement.	13 years old, liked reading.	Courageous in protecting sister, given name of Bluejay. Didn't see mother again for 6 years (i.e. 1868).

Using the notes you have made, write a story about the life of one of these characters. Write this as a first-person narrative as if they were *either* telling parts of their life story to their grandchildren *or* to a stranger interested in finding out about their experiences.

▶ Write about the differences and similarities in culture between the Sioux Indians and the frontier settlers described in this story. As part of your writing:
 – illustrate the importance of love and family ties in both communities
 – explain why you think Sarah enjoyed living with the Sioux and why she felt as she did at the very end of the story
 – why Mary Amanda found it hard to adapt to her new life with the Sioux and why she chose not to return to her mother.

▶ Act out or write the scene in which Sarah is re-united with her mother.

▶ Rewrite as a play script for radio or television – and then act out – any of the scenes in 'Flame on the Frontier'. The scene in which Horse Ears visits Sarah at the end of the story might lend itself particularly well to scripted drama.

The Ugliest of Them All

Before reading

▶ What does the title of this story suggest it may be about? Discuss your ideas in pairs.

▶ Write your own short story of not more than 200 words on this subject. If possible, include an unexpected twist at the end. Read them in groups and comment on how they might be improved.

During reading

▶ Read the story up until the words 'I had to either love or hate her.' (page 34). Predict what the last sentence might be.

After reading

▶ This could be interpreted as quite a depressing story since it dwells only on the things the narrator dislikes about herself – her bad points.
Either: Write about what it is that makes us often dwell on our bad rather than our good points. Express your ideas either as a short story or as a poem.
Or: Under the headings 'Good' and 'Bad' note down your own good and bad points (perhaps as others see you?), then use your notes to do a piece of writing about yourself.

▶ Rewrite the story imagining you are one of the writer's close friends.

▶ Make a tape recording of yourself reading the story or the piece you wrote beforehand. Vary the pitch and pace of your voice to illustrate the mood and interpretation you wish to put across.

▶ 'You never really understand a person until you walk around inside their skin'. This comment is made by the author Harper Lee in her celebrated novel *To Kill A Mockingbird*. Use it as a starting point for group discussion, an individual talk or a piece of writing.

Snapshots of Paradise

> *Before reading*

▶ Work out your own family tree, going back at least three generations to your great-grandparents.

Which relatives do you know well? Which only slightly? Which have you never met but have been told about? Which do you know nothing about? Compare your family tree with that of a friend.

> *During reading*

▶ Note down those aspects of the story – language and places – which suggest an American setting.

▶ Adèle Geras writes very detailed descriptions of people and objects; for example, in the paragraph beginning 'I can't describe it . . . it's strange' (page 52). Note any phrases or sentences which particularly strike you, for use in your own writing.

▶ In this story the main character, Fran, visits her relatives in America for the first time. Below is a family tree of the characters in the story. Look out for them as they appear.

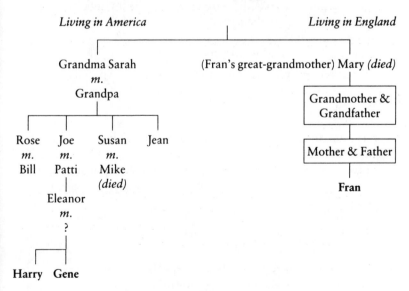

▶ Look out for details of the two brothers, Harry and Gene, which help to build up a picture of their separate characters.

▶ Make notes on the settings and times of the different events and snapshots in the story. Distinguish between 'events' and 'snapshots' by enclosing one in a square. For example:

Fran and Gene talking in garden, waiting for family to gather for snapshot. Early morning.	10.00 am Family group	Fran and Harry talking by the pool. About 11.00 am.	

▶ Write a character study of Gene and Harry in which you compare and contrast their qualities and their faults. Include the following: their appearance; their attitude to Fran; what they say about each other; what other members of the family say about them.

▶ On one level this story is about a holiday romance in which Fran re-examines some of her ideas about love, emotions and relationships. On another level the writer seems to be inviting her readers to question some of their own attitudes to what is important in forming relationships.

Write about what this story means to you.

▶ The story takes place within a single day on a special occasion. Each event is interspersed with a 'snapshot' which focuses in detail on an aspect of the event.

Either: Write about the way the author has chosen to structure the story and the effectiveness of using the 'still' images of photographs to develop the characters and the plot.

(To do this you will need to re-read the snapshot descriptions carefully and also decide why the final snapshot was used to end the story.)

Or: Write a story of your own using a similar structure for the same purpose. If possible, use actual photographs or family snapshots which you can describe in detail and weave into your story.

▶ When Fran returns to England, write her diary of the trip to America, particularly her memories of the family she stayed with. Include reference to how her personal emotions were affected by the visit. Remember to use the first-person narrative voice.

▶ In pairs, read Adèle Geras's personal essay (page 57). What does it add to your appreciation of 'Snapshots of Paradise'? What ideas in it do you find useful for: (a) studying the short story genre and other stories in this collection, and (b) your own personal writing?

▶ Imagine you were given an airline ticket to a country of your choice. Explain where you would choose to go and why.

Debut

Before reading

▶ What does the title of this story suggest it may be about?

▶ What associations does the word 'debut' have for you? If you were making a debut what thoughts would preoccupy you in the hours before it took place?

▶ Can you think of an event or an encounter which has happened to you, and which has changed your opinions and thoughts quite strongly? Talk about this in groups.

During reading

▶ Look out for the reasons the author might have had for choosing the title 'Debut'.

▶ Make a note of the way the author undermines and belittles the boasts and threats the boys make.

▶ 'Her thoughts leaped ahead to the Ball itself' (page 60). Pause at this point and consider Judy's state of mind and anticipations at this moment in the story.

▶ Stop reading at the break in the text after 'She had what they wanted, and the knowledge replaced her shame with a strange, calm feeling of power' (page 66). In pairs, discuss how you think the story will finish.

After reading

▶ Working in pairs decide which of the following statements best sum up the story as a whole. Find examples from the text to back up your choice.

This story is about snobbery and competition.
This story is about pretence and deceit.
This story is about power and ambition.
This story is about sacrifice and hard work.
This story is about social status and identity.
Add some more statements of your own if you wish.

▶ Write a character study of Mrs Simmons. As part of your writing try to get below the surface descriptions given about her in the story and consider why she worked with such 'fierce determination' to launch Judy into 'society'.

▶ Using the following quotation from the story as a starting point, draw up a character study of Judy as she is presented in the story.
   'She had what they wanted, and the knowledge replaced her shame with a strange, calm feeling of power'.
This could be presented as a written piece (with diagrams) or as a talk.

▶ In 'Debut' two alternatives are offered about how girls can cope with insults and personal remarks from boys: ignore them; play them at their own game. What advice would you give?
   Some boys, especially when they are in a group, seem to enjoy trying to make girls feel uncomfortable by making remarks about them. Why do you think such boys behave in this way?
   Write your opinions on these questions. These could form the basis of a group debate.

▶ By the end of the story Judy has learned what her mother has been trying to teach her and treats the 'serious neighbourhood boy', Ernest Lee, with contempt. Compare Judy's expectations and attitudes with those of Fran in 'Snapshots of Paradise'.

The Kestrels

Before reading

▶ What do the title and the first paragraph of this story suggest it may be about?

▶ Adults, especially parents and teachers, sometimes refer to girls and boys as 'a bad influence'. In groups spend a short time building up a checklist of descriptions which they generally use. Next, decide which of these descriptions you consider reasonable and which unreasonable.

▶ The author has chosen to write and structure this story in a particular way: two parallel stories which weave together, written as a third-person narrative. Look out for reasons why the author has written the story in this way; for examples of the way the stories weave together and for reasons why this story is called 'The Kestrels'.

During reading

After reading

▶ In pairs, make notes on the way the story is written and structured. Organise your notes under the column headings below. As a start you may find it helpful to work out which of the five 'example-notes' fits under which heading:

Comment	Story A	Link?	Story B	Comment

1   A girl hitching and finally getting a lift . . .
2   . . . kestrels . . . (title)
3   Time? Late morning? C. thinking back on past events – filling in background?
4   Time? Similar to Story A? Girl caught up in the present – dangers of journey, getting to destination. Girl unnamed – reason?
5   C. out on moors watching kestrels . . .

Using the notes you have made:
Either, write an appreciation of the story as a whole. As part of your writing include ideas and comments on the following:
– the way the story is written and structured
– the development of plot and characters
– reasons for choosing the title
– issues raised by the story (the girls' relationship; parental and school pressures; asserting independence, etc).
Or, write a story of your own in which you experiment with a similar structure and narrative style.

▶ In this story the kestrel seems to have become a symbol to both Claire and Jakey. Describe what this symbol means to you and why the author may have chosen to develop it in the way she did.

▶ Re-write the story as a first-person narrative from either Claire's or Jakey's point of view, or that of Claire's father or mother.

The Application Form

Before reading

▶ Think of some occasions when you have wanted or needed to do something you considered perfectly reasonable and have been prevented by those in authority over you:
  - what have these things been?
  - what has your reaction been?

During reading

▶ Stop reading after the words, 'Brendan expected him to stamp his foot' (page 80). How will each character react to this situation?

▶ Stop reading after the words, 'she did know that there was somebody else, somebody whom she would only have to threaten him with' (page 85). What plan do you think Nell has? Will she be successful?

▶ Look out for the different and sometimes contradictory feelings Nell has for each member of her family.

▶ Make a note of those features of the story which suggest an Irish setting.

After reading

▶ Write a character study of Nell. As part of your writing consider the following points:
  - the things which are important to her
  - the different expectations she has of each member of her family
  - the ways she conforms to and rebels against her role as housewife and mother.

▶ 'The girl was young yet, she would learn. She would come to see how things had to be a certain way, how things were done' (page 84). Write about or discuss in small groups what this quotation means to you, and how far you agree or disagree with it.

▶ It is two years later and Eileen is on the brink of wanting to leave home either to continue her education or to live with her brother and get a job. She, her mother and Brendan have had time to make some changes so that it will not be so difficult for her.

In pairs, consider what these changes might be, then write or improvise the scene which takes place when she breaks the news to her father.

▶ Imagine a few years have passed after the end of the story. Write four short pieces in which each of the characters retells the incident over the application form.

▶ This story raises a number of important issues. For example:
   – the benefits and problems of having an elder sister or brother
   – the different attitudes parents have to their daughters and sons
   – the problems children sometimes have with their parents
   – the problems parents sometimes have with their children.
   Choose one of these as a topic for group debate or a personal piece of writing.

▶ Read Moy McCrory's personal essay (page 88). What does it add to your understanding of 'The Application Form'? What ideas in it do you find useful for: (a) studying the short story genre and other stories in this collection, and (b) your own personal writing?

A Chip of Glass Ruby

Before reading

▶ This story is set in South Africa. Before you begin reading it talk in groups about what you know of the apartheid regime of government and the social and political conditions it imposes on black people. In particular, discuss its implications for their freedom of movement, education, employment and living conditions.
   It is also important to find out about the policies of the present government in South Africa and the ways in which groups opposed to these policies are organising against them.

▶ Have you ever been involved in protesting for or against a particular cause? In groups, talk about motives, actions and feelings shared by those who embrace a cause.

During reading

▶ Note how Nadine Gordimer interweaves domestic and political detail throughout the story. What impact does this have on the reader? What does this contribute to the overall effect of the story?

▶ Make a note of any details which indicate that South Africa is a 'divided country'.

▶ Throughout 'A Chip of Glass Ruby' Mr Bamjee feels that 'his wife was not like other people, in a way he could not put his finger on, except to say what it was not: not scandalous, not punishable, not rebellious. It was, like the attraction that had led him to marry her . . . something he could not see clearly' (page 94).

As you are reading look out for examples which illustrate his incomprehension, and for examples which help him understand his deep-rooted feelings for her.

▶ Stop reading after the second break in the text, which comes after the above quotation (page 94). In pairs discuss how the story has developed so far:
  − the relationship between Mr and Mrs Bamjee
  − Mrs Bamjee's involvement in politics and in the well-being of her family
  − particular lines in the story which strike you as being important.
  Then predict how you think the story will develop.

▶ 'He had become the ghost of a victim, hanging about the scene of a crime whose motive he could not understand and had not had time to learn' (page 99). What do you think is Mr Bamjee's state of mind at this point in the story?

After reading

▶ Write a character study of Mr Bamjee in which you consider the following points:
  − his work
  − his feelings about culture and religion
  − his inability to comprehend his wife's actions
  − his reactions to his wife's arrest
  − his growing understanding of what it is that he admires about his wife.

▶ In pairs decide which of the following statements best sum up the story. Find quotations from the text to back up your choice.
  This story is about strength and perseverance.
  This story is about social divisions and political repression.
  This story is about domestic and family ties.
  This story is about resistance and struggle.
  This story is about knowledge and understanding.
  Add more statements of your own if you wish.

▶ Improvise – and tape – the conversation which takes place between Mrs Bamjee and Girlie on one of the occasions she visits her mother in prison.

▶ Imagine that Mrs Bamjee is tried for her political activities. Write and act out the trial, with characters from the story appearing and being questioned in turn in the witness-box.

Draft the statement that she makes in court to justify her actions. The following extracts from Nelson Mandela's speech to the South African court which sentenced him in 1964 to life imprisonment for 'anti-Government' activities is worth studying for ideas and style:

> Africans want to be paid a living wage. Africans want to perform work which they are capable of doing, and not work which the Government declares them to be capable of. Africans want to be allowed to live where they obtain work, and not be 'endorsed out' of an area because they were not born there. Africans want to be allowed to own land in places where they work, and not to be obliged to live in rented houses which they can never call their own. Africans want to be part of the general population, and not be confined to living in their own ghettos. African men want to have their wives and children to live with them where they work, and not be forced into an unnatural existence in men's hostels. African women want to be with their men folk and not be left permanently widowed in the tribal reserves. Africans want to be allowed out after 11 o'clock at night and not be confined to their rooms like little children. Africans want to be allowed to travel in their own country and to seek work where they want to and not where the Labour Bureau tells them to. Africans want a just share in the whole of South Africa; they want security and a stake in society.

> This then is what the African National Congress is fighting for. Their struggle is truly a national one. It is a struggle of the African people, inspired by their own suffering and their own experience. It is a struggle for the right to live.

> During my lifetime I have dedicated myself to this struggle of the African people. I have fought against white domination, and I have fought against black domination. I have cherished the ideal of a democratic and free society in which all persons live together in harmony and with equal opportunities. It is an ideal which I hope to live for and to achieve. But if need be, it is an ideal for which I am prepared to die.

Turned

Before reading

▶ What does the title of this story suggest it may be about? Think of all the different associations and meanings it could have.

During reading

▶ Read the first two sections of this story down to 'She wept for two' (page 102). In pairs discuss:
   – What you learn about Mrs Marroner: what sort of emotions is she experiencing? Can you guess at what might have caused them?
   – What you learn about Gerta Petersen: why is she feeling as she is? What do you think 'She wept for two' might mean? What is her relationship to Mrs Marroner?

▶ Stop reading at the following points and predict what you think is going to happen next:
   – after 'Then came the deluge' (page 104)
   – after 'Now I can think,' she said (page 106)
   – after 'He let himself in with his latch-key . . . to surprise his wife' (page 108)
   – after 'It was autumn before he found her' (page 110).

▶ This story begins in the present, then moves back and forth between past and present and then on into the future. Look out for the points at which the narrative does this.

After reading

▶ Write brief portraits of the two women in 'Turned'.

▶ Imagine you are either Marion Marroner, Gerta or Mr Marroner. Write an account of your thoughts – on the same night as the story ends – while you are lying in bed before going to sleep.

▶ Continue the story – as narrative or playscript – from its closing words. Add a final paragraph that describes how the life of each character continues in the future.

▶ Write a detailed appreciation of the story, giving as many of your own views as possible. As part of your writing consider the following questions:

- did the opening paragraphs make you want to read on?
- what were your first impressions of the characters? Did you change them as you read on?
- was the structure of the story interesting or confusing?
- why do you think the author chose this structure?
- were you able to predict what was going to happen?
- what did you think about the style and language used?
- was the ending satisfying or annoying? Did it make you reflect further?

▶ Charlotte Perkins Gilman was an American writer at the beginning of this century. Much of her writing concerned the perceptions and experiences of women at that time. How relevant do *you* think the ideas within 'Turned' are today?

Gawain and the Lady Ragnell

| Before reading |

▶ Folk tales, myths and legends are an important part of our child-hood and early years at school. Are there any particular tales you can recall? Why have they stayed in your memory? In groups, share any moral tales or riddles that you remember reading or being told.

▶ In 'Gawain and the Lady Ragnell' a riddle has to be solved, and as in most folk and fairy tales finding out the *correct* answer is *very* important. A king and a brave knight have to find out, 'What is it that women most desire, above all else?'

   In pairs or small groups decide what you think the answer is.

| During reading |

▶ Solving a riddle is a typical ingredient of many folk and fairy tales. While you are reading look out for other typical ingredients. For example:
   - typical characters, situations, events
   - the style in which the story is written
   - the moral the writer is trying to get across
   - the ending.

▶ Stop reading after the words, 'Think carefully before you choose' (page 117). In pairs, predict how you think Gawain will choose.

▶ Folk and fairy tales are usually read to or by young children. From your own knowledge of these stories think about:
  – why this is so
  – the reasons why this story may have been chosen as part of this anthology aimed at older students.

  As part of your discussion you could consider some of the morals you have come across in various folk and fairy tales, and what you think the moral of 'Gawain and the Lady Ragnell' is.

▶ Write an appreciation of the story in which you consider the following points:
  – the ways in which it is similar to other folk and fairy stories
  – the ways in which it differs
  – the qualities in Gawain and Ragnell the writer seems to be praising
  – the moral of the story
  – how successful you think the story is as a whole.

▶ Write your own folk or fairy tale in which you challenge some of the reader's expectations. For example, you could reverse traditional male and female roles or qualities.

The Yellow Wallpaper

▶ Have you read any stories or seen any films which deal with the subject of madness, and how characters seem to become mad or are driven to insanity? Discuss the things which lead to this state of mind and some of the symptoms the characters displayed.

▶ In groups, consider what the author has to say in her accompanying essay about the origins of this short story.

▶ Stop reading after the words, 'So I take pains to control myself – before him, at least, and that makes me very tired' (page 119). In pairs, study this first section carefully.
  – What do you learn about the narrator, her husband and their relationship?

- What do you learn about the house and the room the narrator is in?
- What clues can you find which indicate that all is not well?
- How would you describe the style in which the story is written?
  From the title and your reading of this first section, predict how you think the story will develop.

▶ While you are reading look out for:
- the ways in which the wallpaper increasingly preoccupies the narrator's thoughts
- her descriptions and interpretations of the wallpaper
- details which help create a picture of how she spends her time and what she is doing in the nursery, especially in the last three sections
- how her feelings for her husband and Jennie alter, and vice versa.

After reading

▶ In 'Why I wrote "The Yellow Wallpaper"' the author observes: 'It was not intended to drive people crazy, but to save people from being driven crazy, and it worked' (page 135). Use this as a title for an appreciation of the story and a discussion of your own reactions to it.

▶ Skim-read the story again and write down the descriptions of and words associated with the wallpaper which particularly strike you.
  Using and adapting these, write a poem or lyrical piece of prose about the wallpaper itself in which you try to capture its power and pervasiveness.

▶ Write and act out the scene which took place over dinner when the narrator's mother and Nellie came to visit on the Fourth of July.

▶ Describe the scene which confronted John as he entered the nursery at the end of the story.

▶ Compare and contrast the style and content of 'Turned' and 'The Yellow Wallpaper'. In your writing you could consider the following:
- why the author uses the third-person narrative in 'Turned' and the first-person narrative in 'The Yellow Wallpaper'
- the time-span of each story, and the use of present, past and future
- the feelings and behaviour of Mrs Marroner in 'Turned' and the narrator in 'The Yellow Wallpaper'.

Further ideas for group and individual work

▶ Which characters in the stories did you enjoy reading about or even identify closely with? Write your own story centring on one of these characters, or bring together characters from different stories – for example, Hazel in 'Raymond's Run' and Judy in 'Debut'.

▶ What are your reactions to the ways in which the stories end? Look closely at the concluding lines of each story. If you find the ending unsatisfactory, try rewriting – or acting out – an alternative one.

▶ Some of these stories offer humour to the reader. Look back over the collection and attempt to analyse different writers' use of comedy. You could consider 'Raymond's Run' and 'Snapshots of Paradise'.

▶ 'The Yellow Wallpaper' uses the first-person 'I' narrator to tell the story, while 'Flame on the Frontier' has a third-person narrator observing the action from outside. Which type of narrative device is used in each of the tales? 'Snapshots of Paradise' offers an interesting variation.

What seem to you the advantages and disadvantages of the different types of narrative standpoint? Rewrite sections of any of the stories, changing the narrator's point of view.

▶ Why does someone behave in the way they do? What causes them to take one line of action rather than another? What motivates the characters in these stories? Working in groups, choose one of the stories. Then take it in turns to play the part of one of the characters. Each character is placed in the witness-box and quizzed by the others as to why they behaved as they did in the story. You might start with 'The Application Form' or 'Turned'.

▶ Several of the stories are concerned to put across either a moral or a 'social message'. Write a comparative study of the three tales 'Gawain and the Lady Ragnell', 'Turned' and 'Debut'. Have any of these made you rethink your opinions or beliefs? If so, mention this in your writing.

▶ Many of the characters in these stories face quite difficult decisions and situations. *Choices* have to be made. Discuss how *you* might have reacted in any of these fictional settings.

▶ 'Snapshots of Paradise' uses an interesting narrative technique. Try rewriting one or two of the other stories using the device of 'snapshots' within the narrative.

▶ Mount a dramatised reading – complete with sound effects and music – of one of the stories. This is best practised in small groups and then presented to a larger audience.

▶ Adèle Geras lists seven broad categories of short stories (p. 57). Can you think of any others? Try placing each of the stories in this collection within one of her or your own categories. You can then do the same exercise with other stories you read.

▶ 'A first reading makes you want to know what will happen; a second makes you understand why it happens; a third makes you think.' How true is this in your reading and re-reading of the stories in *Stepping Out*?

Further Reading

Raymond's Run by **Toni Cade Bambara** appears in the collection *Gorilla My Love*. Other short stories by the author appear in *The Seabirds Are Still Alive* (both published by The Women's Press).
Related reading:

The Friends, Rosa Guy, Puffin (1977)
Ruby, Rose Guy, Gollancz (1981)
Edith Jackson, Rose Guy, Puffin (1985)
In The Castle of My Skin, George Lamming, Longman Drumbeat (1979)
The Village By The Sea, Anita Desai, Puffin (1985)

Flame on the Frontier by **Dorothy M. Johnson** was first published in *Indian Country* (André Deutsch). Recommended reading in the same volume is 'A Man Called Horse'.
Related reading:

Indian Tales, Jaime De Angelo, Abacus (1976)
We are Mesquakie, We are One, Hadley Irwin, Sheba (1984)
Sumitra's Story, Rukshana Smith, Bodley Head (1982)
The Woman Warrior, Maxine Hong Kingston, Picador (1981)
Autobiography of a Chinese Girl, Hsieh Ping-Ying, Pandora (1986)
The Chant of Jimmie Blacksmith, Thomas Keneally, Fontana (1984)
Finding A Voice, Amrit Wilson, Virago (1978)

The Ugliest Of Them All by **Stella Ibekwe** first appeared in *Teenage Encounters* (Centerprise).
Related reading:

> *Wasted Women, Friends and Lovers*, Black Ink Collective (1980)
> *So this is England: A Prose Anthology*, Peckham Publishing Project (1984)
> *A Dangerous Knowing: Four Black Women Poets*, Barbara Burford, Gabriela Pearse, Grace Nichols, Jackie Kay, Sheba (1985)
> *Jackie's Story*, Centerprise (1984)
> *Some Grit Some Fire*, Hackney Women Writers, Centerprise (1984)
> *The Collector of Treasures*, Bessie Head, Heinemann (1977)
> *Black Boy*, Richard Wright, Longman (1970)
> *Pure Running*, Louise Shore, Centerprise (1983)

Snapshots of Paradise by **Adèle Geras** has not previously been published in Britain. She has also written a collection of love stories titled *Green Behind the Glass* (Armada Books).
Related reading:

> *More to Life Than Mr Right*, Rosemary Stones (ed.), Piccadilly Press (1986)
> *Meetings and Partings*, Michael Marland (ed.), Longman (1984)
> *It's My Life*, Robert Leeson, Armada (1981)
> *A Sense of Shame*, Jan Needle, Fontana (1980)
> *Breaking Training*, Sandy Weldi, Fontana (1984)
> *Tough Annie*, Annie Barnes, Stepney Books (1980)
> *Your Friend, Rebecca*, Linda Hoy, Bodley Head (1981)

Debut by **Kristin Hunter** was originally published in the United States in the journal *Negro Digest*.
Related reading:

> *Black Lives, White Worlds*, Keith Ajegbo, Cambridge University Press (1982)
> *Green Days by the River*, Michael Anthony, Heinemann (1973)
> *Beka Lamb*, Zee Edgell, Heinemann (1982)
> *The Basketball Game*, Julius Lester, Puffin (1982)
> *Hal*, Jean MacGibbon, Wheaton (1980)
> *In Love And Trouble*, Alice Walker, The Women's Press (1984)

The Kestrels by **Kym Martindale** has been slightly edited for this schools' edition. The complete version was originally published in the collection *The Reach* (Onlywomen Press).

Related reading:

Annie on My Mind, Nancy Garden, Farrar Straus and Giroux (1984)

Dance on My Grave, Aidan Chambers, Pan Horizons (1986)

Faultline, Sheila Ortiz Taylor, The Women's Press (1982)

Inside the Winter Gardens, David Rees (1984)

The Application Form by **Moy McCrory** appears in a collection titled The Water's Edge (Sheba). Another story by Moy McCrory, 'Memento Mori' is in *That'll Be The Day* (Unwin Hyman Short Stories Series).

Related reading:

Nobody's Family is Going to Change, Louise Fitzhurgh, Armada Lions (1978)

It's My Life, Robert Leeson, Armada Lions (1981)

Under Goliath, Peter Carter, Puffin (1977)

My Oedipus Complex, Frank O'Connor, Penguin (1984)

Women's Part. An Anthology of short fiction by and about Irishwomen 1890–1960, Janet Madden-Simpson, Arlen House (1984)

The Female Line. Northern Irish Women Writers, Ruth Hooley (ed.), Universities Press (1985)

A Life of Her Own, Maeve Kelly, Poolbeg Press (1976)

A Chip of Glass Ruby by **Nadine Gordimer** is also available in *The Selected Stories of Nadine Gordimer* (Penguin).

Related reading:

Bandiet: Seven Years in a South African Prison, Hugh Lewin, Heinemann (1982)

Tell Freedom, Peter Abrahams, Faber & Faber (1981)

A Dakar Childhood, Nafissatou Diallo, Longman Drumbeat (1982)

Our Own Freedom. Women in Africa Today, Maggie Murray and Buchi Emecheta, Sheba (1986)

Debbie Go Home, Alan Paton, Penguin (1965)

Wives at War, Flora Nwapa, Tana Press (1980)

No Easy Walk to Freedom, Nelson Mandela, Heinemann African Writer's Series (1965)

A Walk in the Night, Alex La Guma, Heinemann (1968)

Jail Diary of Albie Sachs, David Edgar, Rex Collings (1978)

Part of My Soul, Winnie Mandela, edited by Anne Benjamin, Penguin (1985)

Turned by **Charlotte Perkins Gilman** *is also available in The Charlotte Perkins Gilman Reader* (The Women's Press).
Related reading:

A *Measure of Time*, Rosa Guy, Virago (1984)
The Penguin Dorothy Parker, Penguin (1977)
Brown Girl, Brownstones, Paule Marshall, Virago (1982)
Sula, Toni Morrison, Panther (1982)
My Brilliant Career, Miles Franklin, Virago (1980)
Dubliners, James Joyce, Penguin (1984)
Unwinding Threads: Writing by Women in Africa, Charlotte Bruner (ed.), Heinemann (1985)
Watching Me, Watching You, Fay Weldon, Coronet (1982)

Gawain and the Lady Ragnall by **Ethel Phelps Johnston** also appears in *The Maid of the North* (Holt, Rinehart and Winston). Another collection of tales from the same writer is titled *Tatterhood* (Feminist Press, New York).
Related reading:

S.W.A.L.K., Paula Milne, Thames-Methuen (1983)
The Practical Princess and Other Liberating Fairy Tales, Jay Williams, Macmillan Educational (1986)
Clever Gretchen and Other Forgotten Folk Tales, Alison Lurie, Heinemann (1980)
Girls are Powerful: Young Women's Writings from Spare Rib, Susan Hemmings (ed.) Sheba (1982)
Gregory's Girl in *Act Now* series, Cambridge University Press (1983)
The Handbook of Non-Sexist Writing, Casey Miller and Kate Swift, The Women's Press (1981)
The Kingdom Under the Sea, Joan Aiken, Puffin (1973)

The Yellow Wallpaper by **Charlotte Perkins Gilman** is also available in *The Charlotte Perkins Gilman Reader* (The Women's Press).
Related reading:

The Women of Brewster Place, Gloria Naylor, Sphere Books (1984)
The Color Purple, Alice Walker, The Women's Press (1983)
Portraits, Kate Chopin, The Women's Press (1979)
I Am The Cheese, Robert Cormier, Macmillan Educational (1981)
Slaughterhouse Five, Kurt Vonnegut, Panther (1972)
Second-Class Citizen, Buchi Emecheta, Fontana (1977)